THE JOHN GRAHAM JR. STORY
(From the Archives of a Digger's Son)

By

John Weldon Evans

DEDICATION

To All Past Young Diggers

Who Once Had a Dream

Contents

Prologue

During the latter part of the 19th century, Jamaica was emerging from a slave plantation system into a semi-autonomous colonial system in the British Empire. It was burdened with a struggling economy. The sugar industry had declined due to the loss of cheap slave labor and due to competition from countries like Cuba and Brazil. Even with imported Indian labor, Jamaican landlords still could not maintain their plantations and had to abandon them or face bankruptcy. This gave many liberated Jamaicans the opportunity to move into resulting free villages and squatter towns to attempt to farm these lands on their own, but they could not make it profitable due to low market prices for their crops, floods, severe droughts, and other forms of hardships. Generally, the entire Jamaican labor population was experiencing very high unemployment, poverty, and hard times. As a result, able-bodied Jamaicans started leaving their country in masses to go abroad to find work to sustain themselves and their families. There was an exodus to places like Panama, Cuba, and Brazil. So, it was not strange that foreign enterprises had no difficulty attracting workers from Jamaica and, later, Barbados and other Caribbean islands. The Americans started recruiting in 1850 for workers to build their 50-mile Panama Railroad; the French did massive recruiting in Jamaica in the 1870s to find labor to attempt to build a sea-level Panama Canal (though they failed); and the Americans, after buying out the bankrupt French in 1903, did massive recruitment in Barbados and in other Caribbean islands for labor to build a six-lock, 50-mile Panama Canal across the Isthmus; also, the United Fruit Company did recruitment in the Caribbean islands for labor to build a huge sugar plantation in Cuba after Cuba won its independence from Spain in the early 1900's. Many workers from all over the Caribbean islands also went on their own to these high labor-demanding places to find work.

Among the more than 70,000 Jamaicans, Barbadians, and other Caribbeans who left home under contract or on their own to work on the construction of the Isthmian Railway, the French Panama Canal, and the U. S. Panama Canal between 1850 and 1914, there were countless stories of struggles, hardships, and tragedies. A great many Caribbeans lost their lives in Panama due to disasters, terrible accidents, and diseases during the construction of two of the most ambitious and hazardous enterprises, the Panama Railroad and the Panama Canal. While many who survived chose to remain on the Isthmus of Panama and continue their life journey there, many decided to return to their countries of origin to live out the remainder of their lives. In most, if not all, cases, they had very little or nothing to show for their sacrifices except for scars, sad memories, and bitter stories. Here is one of such stories taken from the archives of that past era. It is the story of a young, innocent, unfledged, but eager teenager who left his home in Jamaica during the peak years of the United States construction of the Panama Canal to join his father and uncle and the adventures he experienced. Five years had such an impact on his young, untarnished life that it was remarkable how he managed to survive and how severely his life had changed as a result. But I'll let the readers judge that for themselves in the following journey with our young adventurer.

Chapter I: A Trench Pen Boy's Dream Comes True

Sitting on the balcony at home in Trench Pen, John Graham, Jr. was sipping on some berry juice when Aunt Sarah approached on her return home from downtown Kingston.

"I got something for you," she said to him, "a letter came from Panama from your father. I got it right here in my hand. Come, let's go inside and see what it says."

They went inside, and Sarah called to her sister Beulah to come to join them and hear what John Graham, Sr. had to say from Panama. As they gathered around the kitchen table, Sarah opened the letter, and as she did so, something fell out of the envelope onto the floor. She picked it up, and, lo and behold, it was what John Graham, Jr. had been suffering so long for; it was a one-way ticket to Panama for him to sail on the S.S. San Jose on November 30, 1910, two weeks from that day. The letter said:

Panama City
November 12, 1910

Dear Sarah and Beulah,

It is a fine day today in Panama; the rains are slacking off a bit, and the weather is getting a little more pleasant these days. Your brother, Cyrus, sends you his regards and he says he will write to you soon. I send you and Beulah all my love, hoping that all is well with you both and with my eager beaver son. Please go to the cable office in Kingston and get the money I sent to help you and Beulah take care of him. That said, in this letter, you will find a ticket for John Jr. to come join me in Panama now that he has reached 17 and can find work here to help him financially and to help you

1

and Beulah, seeing as how you are the only family he has left in Jamaica after his mother, Muriel, passed away.

I know you already took care and got all John's papers in order over there since you've been working on it for some time, so his passport and documents are in order to travel on the date the ticket says. So, I will be waiting to meet him here at the pier in Colon when he arrives. Thank you, God bless you, and may all of you keep well now.

Love,
John Graham, Sr."

After reading the letter, Sarah turned to John.

"I know you are happy as a lark now since all you've been dreaming about is going to Panya country to dig the canal with your father. Well, your dream has come true at last."

She showed him the ticket and he looked at it to make sure it was real. He was so happy! Every day he had been dreaming about going to Panama when oftentimes, in his daydreams, it was Aunt Beulah's voice that would return him back to the here and now.

"Yes," said Beulah as she woke him up again out of his favorite reverie, "and I hope when you go there, you don't forget about us, and you write and let us know how you are getting along."

Sarah and Beulah lived in a little house their parents had built and left for them when they went to be with the Lord. Sarah was the eldest of four Graham children and worked as a cook in a downtown Kingston restaurant. Beulah, the youngest, was a seamstress, a trade she learned from her mother and from her aunt. Cyrus was the second eldest who became a mason and a carpenter by trade. John, Sr. was a master carpenter like his father, and his son, John, Jr., followed in his footsteps.

The two sisters eked out a living with the help of their two brothers, who, like many Jamaicans at the time, had left to find work in Panama, and John, Jr. would help around the house cleaning up and doing a little carpentry work because he, too, was handy with a hammer and with his hands (like his father and grandfather.) He would often hang around the kitchen when Aunt Sarah or Beulah was cooking, and they didn't mind showing him how to handle himself in the kitchen preparing a few dishes.

"You better learn to cook for yourself," said Aunt Sarah, "or else you are going to starve, you hear me now. Don't say we never teach you." And he paid close attention to what they taught him. John Jr. was now a young teenager, and he had finished the Colonial primary school for children descended from former slaves. He had received primary education in reading, writing, arithmetic, religion, agriculture, and manual arts and had excelled, especially in carpentry and woodwork. There was little to do in Kingston, and after he completed his primary school education, his dream was to go and live with his father in Panama.

When the news came from Panama, he was so happy all he could think about was the great adventure that awaited him, about pulling his own weight alongside his father, about moving earth, bringing down mountains, taking on nature and the elements, being a digger, being his own man.

"Yes, Panama, here I come," were his thoughts as he prepared for the upcoming sea voyage two weeks from the day the letter came from Panama.

When that day finally came, November 30, 1910, Aunts Sarah and Beulah were there at the pier to see him off. They hugged and kissed him.

"We're going to miss you, don't forget to write now, don't forget about us," said his aunts as they waved him goodbye.

Chapter II: A Mild Sea Sickness and Arrival in Colon

The ship was almost out of sight of Kingston when John Graham Jr. was standing on the deck leaning onto the rail, and he began to feel his stomach turning like something inside wanted to escape every time the ship pitched and rolled with the ocean waves. He never felt that way before, and it made him buckle a little bit. A stranger standing nearby noticed his discomfort.

"Is this your first trip at sea, young man?"

John tried to fight back the squirming feeling as he braced himself and shook his head in the affirmative.

"The bad feeling in your stomach will soon pass," reassured the stranger, "It happened to me, too, on my first sea voyage. If it gets any worse, you can always go and see the ship's physician for some temporary remedy. Where are you heading to, son?" asked the stranger.

John turned towards the stranger. Somehow, he didn't look like any 3rd class passenger or unemployed job seeker but rather like a seasoned traveler or a businessman on a routine voyage.

"To Panama," answered John Graham, Jr. "I am going to meet my father and get a job like him working on the Panama Canal."

"Is that so? As it turns out, I am going to Panama myself, but not to work on the Panama Canal; I work for the United Fruit Company. You ever heard of the United Fruit Company?"

"No, sir," said John. "I haven't."

"They are a very big company, son, all over the islands. Why this very ship you are on is owned by them. They have dozens and dozens of steamships that travel all over the world and carry their goods and passengers; it is called "the Great White Fleet." And they own a good part of Central America and the Caribbean. They ship produce that is grown in the Caribbean, like sugar, banana, rum, coconuts, coffee, cocoa, and all kinds of tropical fruits everywhere on their shipping line. I know you have seen men who worked in the banana and sugar plantations in Jamaica, haven't you now?"

"I don't know, perhaps, but many of them have been unemployed lately, so I hear my aunties say, because there isn't any work in Jamaica, and all the plantations have practically gone out of business."

"Yes, that may be true for Jamaica, but there are other places where the sugar and banana business is doing quite well, like Cuba, for instance, and Brazil, and even parts of Panama like Bocas Del Toro and Almirante. If the workers can travel to other places, they can find work, just like how you and many men who are going to Panama to work on the Canal. You got to go where the jobs are available if you want to work."

"You say you work for this United Fruit Company; what is your job exactly?" asked John.

"I am an employment agent for the U.F.C. I hire workers and advertise jobs for the company wherever the jobs are available. My name, by the way, is Samuel R. Brewster, travel agent and employment manager, and here is my business card. I have an office in Colon on Front Street.

"And my name is John Graham, Jr. Like I said, I am going to Panama to work on the Canal with my father."

"I know you said that, young man, but something you've got to learn is you have to know more than one trade or kind of job to survive in this life. In case one doesn't work out, you always got another one to fall back on."

"I suppose you are a good example of that, with all due respect to you, sir?"
"I sure am. You see, I am also an insurance salesman, and I once worked on the Canal when the French were running it. And right now, I am thinking of going into the real estate business in Panama City or Colon. Never put all your eggs into one basket, son. Always learn to do more than one thing in life. By the way, how's the stomach feeling now? Any better?"

"Much better, thank you."

"You see, all you needed was some good conversation."

And with that, they parted company, Mr. Brewster going to his first-class accommodation and John to his third-class cabin, which he shared with two others. John and Mr. Brewster would not see each other again for the rest of the voyage.

The S.S. San Jose, a United Fruit Company steamer, sailed into Limon Bay, Colon, on the morning of December 2, 1910. Already anchored in the docks were a French merchant ship, a steamer with a German flag, and a UFC Royal Mail Steamer that was unloading passengers and cargo onto the pier. John Graham, Jr. stood on the deck, taking in the scene of the harbor filled with Indians and locals in canoes or "cayukas" swarming aboard a steamboat whose chimney was belching forth smoke. The Indians and local workers were trafficking in coconuts, ivory nuts, and bananas with which their cayukas were laden.

As the San Jose was unloading its passengers and cargo, John looked frantically at the shore to see if he could recognize the one person he had hoped would be there to meet him, his father. In the harbor house, he was not there either, and after John had cleared the port immigration authorities, his father was still nowhere to be seen. He was alone in this strange place as he was exiting the port building, and just as he was about to lose all hope, a tall, middle-aged West Indian man touched him on the shoulder.

"Are you John Graham's son?"

He had the same name as his father and turned towards his greeter, a little surprised.

"Yes, I am, but where is my father? He promised he would be here to meet me."

"Your father could not come. I promised him I would come in his place. I am your uncle, Cyrus Graham. I left Jamaica when you were a little baby, and several years later, your father came and joined me here in Panama. Let me help you with your things; we'll walk to the train station, which isn't far from here, and then we will ride the train to Panama City, where your father and I live. I'll explain everything to you later."

They walked east on 13th Street to Front Street and turned north toward the railroad station. Since the train for Panama City was not departing for another hour or so, they decided to walk a couple of short blocks and buy some cool drinks and fruits from the vendors along 13th Street near Bolivar.

There were street vendors everywhere selling coconuts, bananas, plantains, avocado pears, lottery tickets, etc. There was a peanut vendor with a peanut stove, which was seen along the sidewalk just outside a fruit shop, making a funny musical sound with its whistle as it let off steam. Hand carts and horses and buggies were everywhere, and vendors were trying to catch all the tourists from off the ships and other people walking by. As they walked toward Bolivar Avenue, Uncle Cyrus did most of the talking.

"Son, what a difference a few years can make!"

"What do you mean?" asked John.

"The last time I was here in this Colon city, it was nothing like it is now. It has improved so much that I hardly recognize it. The Americans really did a good job cleaning it up. Colon was a "death trap," as it was called back in the late 80s when the French were here. Thank heavens the mosquitos are gone, the diseases are gone, the streets are clean, and everywhere is disinfected. You couldn't even get clean drinking water until they built a reservoir to supply clean running water. They built a sewerage system, too, or we'd be walking in filth right now, and they built decent pavements. I tell you, son, you wouldn't have been able to set foot in this place eight or nine years ago. It's a good thing you came now. God knows how you would have survived back then. Anyway, even your father wasn't here yet to see it, and I don't think you were more than a little tot at that time."

They stopped at a corner vendor stand and purchased fresh coconut water, some banana fritters, and roasted peanuts roasted on a peanut stove run by the same fruit vendor. There wasn't enough time for them to look for a sit-down restaurant to have a decent meal, so while they were eating what they bought from the stand, Uncle Cyrus prompted John to finish quickly and take what he couldn't finish with him to eat on the train.

"Let's go," he said. "If we are going to catch the noon train, we'd better be going now." And they started back toward the station.

They boarded the train at 11:50 a.m. and sat in the second-class (colored) section, which on a Saturday had a fair number of passengers traveling to Panama City. The journey across the Isthmus then took about two hours, and, for a while, the sights and scenes attracted the attention of John Graham, Jr. They were traveling through the tropical bush and forest land at first; then they came to towns along the construction sites. As they passed the town of Gatun, they saw some signs of civilization alongside the route. They saw a few vendors squatting on the ground and, beside them, a stand of bananas. There were some shanties in the background, and on some of them were crudely written: "Billiard Saloon," "Barber's Shop," and "Cool Drinks." Up on a hill, there was a little town; then they saw some bungalows standing on stilts that must be the homes where the work crew live. Not far away, on the opposite side, in a valley, there were massive concrete walls rising 80 or 90 feet from the ground.

"Those must be the great locks they are building," said Cyrus. "In a few more years, all that area will be filled with water, and the canal will be finished, and it is men like your father and me who will have built it with our backs and hard labor."

"What is the kind of work you and my father do in the Canal?" asked John.

"John, your father worked as a carpenter. He helped build the scaffolds, the buildings, bungalows, and anything you see made of wood in the Canal Zone. As for me, I am a "digger" and drill operator. I drill deep holes in hard rocks so they can pour in the dynamite to blast open the mountainside and to loosen the earth so the men and steam shovels can remove it. Most of the time, though, it's the men who carry the dynamite and the wiremen who do the most dangerous work of blasting away the mountainsides because they carry the dynamite on their shoulders, and the wiremen lay the charges -- many men lose their lives doing that kind of work."

"Uncle Cyrus?"

"Yes," replied Cyrus.

"Can you tell me now why my father didn't come to meet me in Colon? Is he sick or something?"

"No, John. It is a hard thing for me to tell you this, but he is your father, and you have a right to know. The truth is, your father had a heart attack and died while you were at sea on your way to Colon. I am sorry to have to tell you this, son. He went to sleep three nights ago and never woke up. We shared an apartment together, and the next morning, when he did not awaken, I called him several times, but he could not hear me. He was gone."

And a sadness came into his eyes as he told John, and you could feel his pain for losing his only brother. John, in the meantime, remained quiet and stared into space, trying to hold back the tears as he realized he would never see his father alive again. He'll never be able to show his father how much he had grown these past 6 years, how good he had become with tools just like him; they'll never get to work side by side as he had imagined; now he'll never get to hear his father's tales of his experiences or hold his hands and share with him his own dreams that he had been dreaming back in Kingston about future father-and-son adventures.

Thinking about all the things that they would never get to do in this life together made him very sad. He started to feel the pain like his uncle, and they both became very quiet, and neither spoke another word for a long time. After a while, John closed his eyes and fell asleep and did not awaken until Uncle Cyrus shook him and told him they had reached Panama City.

Chapter III: Settling Down in Caledonia with Uncle Cyrus

When they disembarked at the station, the last stop on the Colon-Panama line, they headed north on Central Avenue and didn't have far to walk to reach their destination.

"There's the building up ahead!" said Uncle Cyrus.

"Which one is it, Uncle Cyrus?"

"You see that three-story building on the right just up ahead of you? That's where your Dad and I live. It's probably the most famous building ever built in Panama City. It was built by a German named Carlos Muller, son of Oscar Muller, a European who had returned to settle in Panama after being disillusioned by the California gold rush adventure."

As he said that, his nephew interrupted him.

"What do you mean, Uncle Cyrus? What is the Gold Rush adventure?"

"Son, that's a long story. That's one of the reasons that got all these Americans coming down here in the first place. You see, somebody found some gold in the earth in California, and because of it, there was a wild rush of people trying to go there to dig for gold, but they couldn't easily get to California. They couldn't travel across the United States by land from east to west because of mountains, wilderness country, no good roads, and mainly because of dangerous Indians who would attack them. So, it was easier to take a ship from N.Y. to Colon, take the train in Colon and travel south to Panama City by rail, and then take a ship from Balboa port to California."

"That's a lot of trouble to go through just to dig for gold."

"Well, you know, John, that's what drives the white man crazy, gold. Anyway, let me get back to Mr. Carlos Muller and the Muller building. As I was saying, when he came from California, he went into real estate and bought a tract of land here in Caledonia from the Panama Railroad Company, who owned most of the real estate, and he built the largest residential wooden structure ever built in Panama that is made up of 76 apartments on the upper floors (the street level reserved for commercial business). Casa Muller, or "Mullah building," as we West Indians call it, was built primarily to accommodate the large numbers of West Indians who work on the Canal Zone and are in urgent need of housing. Your father and I were very fortunate when we were looking to move from Culebra, and a lodge brother told us about this new building that was just finished, and they were looking to rent to West Indians who work on the Canal. As consumers, we are the main source of spending large amounts of cash in Panama City. They need our silver money badly. We are the largest population in this district of Caledonia, as well as in Maranon, San Miguel, and El Chorrillo. And it's the best place we could find, too. It's perfect, centrally located and all. Everything is nearby: the railroad, the Caledonia market, Central Avenue, and they will soon finish building brand new tram cars to run on Central Avenue all the way to the Canal Zone. As you will find out for your self, many West Indians even own bars or cantinas, little cook shops, and stores, barbershops, and stands in the neighborhood. There are churches, too, like the Christian Mission Baptist Church, St. Paul's Episcopal Church, and The Salvation Army Church in Washapali, and there are many other gathering places and social halls like the Jamaican Society Hall and the Elks Hall that we Caribbean people frequent."

John was taking it all in as he got a firsthand education from his uncle.

"Here we are," said Uncle Cyrus as they reached the front entrance to the Mullah building. "Watch your step now. We got to climb up one flight of stairs to the apartment."

Muller Building (Google)

As they entered Muller's building, which stretched the length of 22nd, 23rd, and 24th streets on Central Avenue, they walked up one flight to the second floor to an apartment overlooking Central Avenue.

"This is where we live, your father and me," said Cyrus. "We shared this 3-room apartment after we moved from Culebra. I had lived in Colon when the French were there in the 1880s, and I was glad to leave that "death trap," though Culebra wasn't any better. In 1904, when your father came to the Isthmus, we stayed together in Culebra near the work site for a while, then we moved here to Caledonia, where we rented this place, which by comparison is a lot better."

After unpacking his luggage, John was shown his space, which was where his father slept and kept his personal belongings when he was alive.

On the walls of the apartment, there were pictures of several people: his father with Uncle Cyrus and friends at a social gathering, a picture of the worksite and work crew, individual photographs of his father and uncle, and his mother when she was alive, a blurred photograph of his grandparents, aunts, and uncles.

"Those are some of your family," said his uncle as he noticed John examining the pictures. "Do you recognize anyone?"

"Yes," said John, "There's my mother. She died when I was three. I still dream about her sometimes. And this here is Aunt Sarah and Aunt Beulah, and this is Grandma Graham before she died. I knew them all in Jamaica, but I never met my grandfather."

"No, you couldn't have," said Cyrus. "He died about the time when you were just born. Hard labor killed him before his time, as it did many good men of his day. Maybe with your generation or with your children's generation, things will be different. Anyway, to change the subject, there are a few things we must get done before today is over. First, I am going to fix something for us to eat, and then I'll take you with me to go see about the arrangements for tomorrow for your father's burial. Everything is already settled, but I just want to review the final arrangements and also introduce you to some people."

By "some people," he meant the people who were handling the burial -- John, Sr. used to pay monthly dues to a death benefit association that would pay for his burial expenses. Cyrus also wanted him to meet some lodge people who were serious about doing their secret ceremony for the dead before releasing him for burial. Fortunately for john Graham junior's father, he died in bed; otherwise, it would have been hard if he had died on the construction site in Culebra Cut. Then they might never have been able to find his body, like so many who are still scattered in the rubble beneath landslides forever or blown to bits in the gravely hillside terrain.

When they reached the Lodge Hall, he was glad to see one of his lodge brothers, Robert Cox, whom he and his brother John had known from back home and who used to work in Culebra. He took a job in Pedro Miguel and moved to "P" Street, not far from Central Avenue. On several occasions, shortly after they arrived home from work, Robert would drop by the apartment and invite them, especially on Friday evenings, to come with him and some other friends to assemble at a social cantina on Central Avenue. Although they weren't heavy drinkers, for friendship's sake, they would agree to show up at the bar where they would meet some other friends from back home. Sometimes, on Saturdays, they would also run into each other at Walter Grant's barber shop on Central Avenue and 24th Street.

"Cyrus, yuh old "buggar" yuh, yuh got back just in time," said Robert as he greeted him. "Is this young man yuh nephew, John Graham's son?"

"Yes, you can see he's almost a man now. All seventeen years of him and growing tall like his father. He is John Graham, Jr."

"John, this is Robert Cox, the lodge gate keeper and a good friend of your father and me.

"Hi, John Graham's son; sorry about yuh father, but he is in a better place now."

"Thank you, sir," replied John Jr.

"Bob, is the ceremony started yet?" asked Cyrus.

"Yes, it has."

"Can we go inside?"

"As a lodge brother, you can go inside and participate, but although he is John Graham's son, he is not yet initiated, and he will have to wait in the outside waiting area till it's over. I hope for his sake he can take it while he hears the goings on and not get scared, though. Young man, yuh not scared now, are yuh, son?"

"Me scared? No, I'll be alright. I'm more scared of the living than the dead. Besides, it's my own father; why would I be scared?"

And that remark so impressed the gatekeeper, Robert Cox, that he said not another word to him.

John was not afraid. In fact, he later showed interest in joining the Freemasons Lodge, and sure enough, Uncle Cyrus would make sure he became an apprentice member. The next day, Sunday, December 4, 1910, the funeral took place just a few miles outside of the city in Corozal Cemetery, where most deceased West Indian workers are buried. It was well attended by friends and co-workers of John Graham, Sr., and the very high attendance was helped by the fact that it was on a Sunday.

One day, a month or so after the funeral, Uncle Cyrus took John, Jr. to a gathering at the lodge hall where a visiting high-ranking officer of the black Freemasons from the U. S. was giving a speech about the history and challenges of black lodges in the U. S. After the formalities and introduction, he greeted the audience and delivered the following speech.

"It might come as no surprise to many of you in this audience that in the United States and in most places (which is probably everywhere the white man controls), white lodges do not even entertain the thought of a black man being allowed to join their organization. Racism prevails in all venues of our society, even in lodges and churches. However, because of determined and inspired black leaders like Prince Hall, who in the year 1784, with fourteen other Blacks in the Boston African American community, after being rejected by the white masonic lodges, founded their own Grand Lodge of Freemasonry, and was granted a charter by England, thereby establishing the first African Lodge, No. 459. As these black lodges grew in number, they sometimes referred to them as the Prince Hall Freemasons and Fraternal organizations. After that, Freemasonry began to spread far and wide throughout the world, including here in Panama.

A similar history was true with the Odd Fellows Lodge when, in 1843, a man named Peter Ogden and a group of other blacks petitioned the Manchester American Oddfellows to allow them to join, and they were denied membership because of their color. Peter Ogden, a black sailor, then convinced the group to petition England's Liverpool Grand United Order's governing body, and thus, they were able to form their own lodge #644. The American white lodges refused to recognize them for the same reason: they were black. Peter Ogden and his group, therefore, changed their name to: "The Grand

United Order of Odd Fellows," which named black affiliates from then on.

The black man, therefore, because of these and other rejections, has had to form his own fraternal organizations, and just as well that we have our own African Freemasons, Foresters Friendly Society, our own United Order of Oddfellows, Improved Benevolent and Protective Order of the Elks of the World (IBPOE) lodges and others. We do not need to be where we are not wanted, and we will not practice reverse discrimination either.

"We will practice the true meaning of fraternity and brotherly love with all who are willing to join us in that endeavor."

The speaker continued to laud the efforts of the Panamanian Freemasonry Lodge as well as other black fraternal organizations and offered compliments and well wishes from the home organization in the U.S. After his speech, there were other speakers and presentations, and it went on into the late evening. Uncle Cyrus did not stay for the end of the program, and he and John Jr. left to go home to get an early start in the morning.

Anyway, after considering whether to join the equally popular IBPOE (Improved Benevolent and Protective Order of Elks) lodge at the time or the Freemasons, it was the African Freemason lodge Uncle Cyrus and John Graham, Sr. decided to join and which John Graham, Jr., with Uncle Cyrus' sponsorship, also joined. It was good in those days to be a member of a fraternity, and John was proud of his membership like a badge of honor. He learned some of the secret signs and codes and ways of communicating, and he learned respect for the fraternity and swore to live up to the oath of the order: "to show brotherly love and affection, to practice charity towards all those in need and facing adversity and to treat them as equals; to show tolerance and respect for others; to care for the sick, orphans, the elderly and the homeless, etc."

Of course, John and Uncle Cyrus wrote home and told Aunt Sarah and Aunt Beulah about their brother's passing. The

Sunday after John's arrival, his father was buried in Corozal cemetery on a hill where silver workers are buried, and the little savings he had, and any death benefit amounts forthcoming from the lodge and the fraternity and society he belonged to, were forwarded to the sisters by Uncle Cyrus. John Jr., with Uncle Cyrus's help, was able to take care of himself, and, in fact, he wasted no time adjusting to his new environment.

It was a good time of the year to be in Panama except for the passing of his father, John Graham, Sr. Christmas holidays were approaching, and every West Indian household, candy shop, cook shop, little market, church, and lodge that existed came alive with the Christmas spirit. All the stands were loaded with Jamaican treats such as fruit cakes, sorrel, chutney, rum cakes, Christmas puddings, black sorrel drinks, rum punch, ginger beer, souse and pickled pig feet, black pudding, regular curry goat, and curry chicken. You could hear plenty of Christmas music and calypsos playing on the radios and people speaking Jamaican-type patois. It was certainly an ideal time for him to assimilate into the new environment. It made him feel like he was back home in Jamaica somehow.

Of course, Christmas soon passed, and reality set in. He had to find work, but no matter, Uncle Cyrus had that covered.

It was in the first week of January 1911, on a Sunday evening, when Cyrus reminded him.

"Tomorrow, Monday morning, we're going to meet the white boss and get you a j-o-b."

Chapter IV: Working on the Panama Canal

Monday morning, along with numerous other diggers, he and Uncle Cyrus took the labor train going down the line to the work site. When they reached Culebra, John saw for the first time the monstrous Gold Hill and Contractor's Hill and the men all along the two mountainsides and in the valley at work moving dirt and singing chanteys:

> "Come on boys, hear the corchee blowing,
> John Crow today, today.
> Look down the track and see the straw boss coming,
> John Crow today, today.
>
> Pick up yuh picks and shovels in yuh hand,
> John Crow today, today.
> We're going to work for Uncle Sam,
> John Crow today, today..."
>
> When we get paid, we gwine drink gin,
> John Crow today, today.
> If it doesn't make you fat, it will make you thin,
> John Crow today, today.

The sledgehammer crew had a chantey, too, that went as follows:

> Ten poun hammer kill me partner,
> Somebody's dying every day.
> Ten poun hammer kill my partner,
> Somebody's dying every day.
> Watah boi come gimme some watah,
> Somebody's dying every day.
> Ten poun hammer kill my partner,
> Somebody's dying every day.

Digging in Culebra (Google)

And this would continue rhythmically while the digging and the drilling and hammering went on in unison, and the dirt started to fly, and the stubborn rocks soon were all pulverized.

All the work gangs would join in from one chantey to another all day long to make the work easier and bearable.

Cyrus approached the headman in charge.

"Boss," said Uncle Cyrus, "this here is my nephew; he is John Graham's son, John Graham, who died last week. Can you give him a job, Boss? He is healthy and strong and willing to work hard."

"We can use another helper," said the white boss, "Let him go and see the timekeeper and put him to work right away. You're a good man, Cyrus; it is no problem for me to give your nephew a job. When he is finished with the timekeeper, let him join the other helpers who will show him what to do."

John was hired at 8 cents an hour helping the work crew by bringing water to them and doing lighter duties as needed, which means he was right there in the thick of the hustle and bustle and rumbling and tumbling and shouting and roaring and laughing and chantey singing from day to day.

Even after work, when they came home, he and Uncle Cyrus joined in with other workers as they socialized in the cantinas or in Grant's barber shop along Central Avenue, and he heard them carrying on about the dangers on the canal, it never seemed to faze him a bit.

"Did you hear what happened in '08 down in Bas Obispo?" asked one of the workers sitting in the bar.

"No, tell us what happened," said the others who had never worked in the Gorgona site.

"On the morning of Dec. 12, 1908, at 11:10 a.m., 21 tons of dynamite suddenly exploded, killing 23 workers and injuring 40 others. The evidence of the terrible force was seen as pieces of flesh and bones were turned over with picks and shovels. The charge consisted of 51 holes 60 feet deep, spreading over a larger territory. It was a chain reaction when the charge in the last hole went off by accident, and the concussion caused the other 50 charges to explode.

Had a labor train filled with 500 laborers passed by just a few minutes later, that train, which was still in view of the explosion, would have also been blown to bits, killing 500 more. There were all kinds of rumors afterward, one claiming that it was the "powder man" who had been drinking the night before or it was acidic water from the earth that seeped into the dynamite and caused the explosion, but they couldn't be sure what really caused it. The victims of 90% of all deaths due to accidents in Culebra are West Indians."

"That was terrible," said another worker, "and you were there when this happened?"

"Yes, I was," said the first worker, "but not close enough, obviously, or I wouldn't be here now telling you about it."

Then, a third worker joined in the conversation.

"This Canal digging is a very dangerous business, that's true. I remember in 1909, I saw men working on the scaffolding for the locks 8 stories high without safety harnesses. They were crazy to do that job without safety harnesses. I saw a few good men get killed when the scaffold became unhooked, and they fell, and the scaffold above them fell upon them, killing them."

And yet another man jumped into the conversation with his comments.

"If yuh ask me if me gwine dig me gwine dig high up on the hilltop. They down in the bottom got nowhere fe run when dirt and rock start come tumbling down pon them."

Some of them sitting in the bar thought this was funny and started to laugh, but alcohol would make men say anything crazy. Another one more serious added his contribution.

"It might seem funny to some o yuh, but yuh know how many landslides occur in that canal and will continue to occur as long as man keeps fooling with nature? In 1907 alone, there were more than a dozen slides, and I think it was in October of that year there was the biggest landslide in Cucaracha not far from Culebra that caused 500,000 cu. Yds. of the earth to come sliding down like a glacier from the North Pole, and it kept up for 14 days straight without stopping. Fortunately, I don't think anybody was killed in that one, although it stopped the digging for a while, and they had to bring dozens and dozens of steam shovels to clear that one up."

"Anyway," said a fifth worker, "we all know there is danger in the work we do, and maybe some of us will go out in the morning and never come home in the evening, but we do it because we got to do it to survive. Mostly, it is careless people who don't use their heads that cause these accidents anyway. If we are careful, most of us will get through and bring bread home to feed our families. In any case, there's a young greenhorn among us who just started working two or three months in the ditch. This kind of talk yuh talking goin' scare the hell out of him, so why yuh don't change the subject. Let's talk 'bout something else, women or some ting spicy, for instance."

And they agreed, even though one of them insisted:

"He shouldn't be in the bar anyway. He is underage. Maybe the laws in Panama are not strict, but back home, he wouldn't be allowed in a bar with grown men until he reached 21. Bet he is no more than 17 or 18."

At that point, Uncle Cyrus jumped in and let them know he was with him, and they were leaving anyway, so they didn't have to worry anymore. And he and John left the bar and went home. Uncle Cyrus knew they were right, though, and he said to John:

"That's the last time I'm taking you inside a bar 'till you reach of age. Your father wouldn't approve of it either. I'm sure of that."

The next morning was the start of the work week, and it would mark the fifth month of his employment. So far so good, he had not witnessed any disasters so far, although, on several occasions, he had seen blasting going on that sent smoke billowing and rocks flying, "Fire in the hole," one man would shout, and everybody, including himself, took cover a safe distance away from the explosion. It was exciting to him to see the drama played out each time; it seemed like fun. But all that changed one day. It was after lunch, nine months after he was on the job working as a helper on Snake Mountain when he got the first up-close experience that scared him out of his skin. The man who laid the dynamite was just talking to him during lunchtime just a few minutes ago, talking and laughing, and even offered him half of his sandwich.

"Young fella, watch yuh self and be careful out here if yuh want to live a long life," he had said to John, "and don't ever go near that dynamite, yuh hear."

Strange advice came from him, who held the dynamite in his hands every day like it was nothing. John was just about to take some water to the men at the bottom of the hill when he heard the white boss shouting.

"Tell that damn fool to get out of there! He's trying to get himself killed!!"

And he heard some other men yelling.

"Get back!! Get back!!"

And then it happened. The same man who laid the dynamite sticks was fool enough to turn back to see if he had set the charge right because the dynamite didn't go off like it was supposed to; he wanted to make sure. Too late! As he got within 2 feet, the blast went off so loud and strong it sent pieces of his body parts flying in all directions. There was nothing anyone could do after that, and after a few minutes, the white boss hollered.

"All right, get back to work and clean that mess up!! We got a schedule to meet!!"

John couldn't believe what he had just seen and was shaking all over.

"Little John, he sure got his feet wet today," said one worker.

"Look at him," said another worker, "he is shaking like a leaf."

"He's a real veteran now," said another, "Bet they goin' give him a pick and shovel now and a real man's pay to dig dirt and maybe lay some dynamite, too!"

And they laughed and tried to make jokes at John's expense.

It wasn't all that funny to John Graham, Jr., though, who barely finished the day's work in one piece. When he went home that evening, he spoke to his uncle.

"Uncle Cyrus, I don't think I want to work on the Canal anymore. Today was my last day."

"What made yuh change yuh mind, John? Is it the talk in the bar the other night?"

"No, Uncle, I guess I was all wrong about the Canal. I thought it would be a great and exciting adventure, but it is not. Uncle, with my own two eyes, I see a man's head blown off today, and the sad part is I was just sharing a sandwich and talking with him a few minutes earlier during lunchtime. I can still see his face in my mind. I'll never go back on that mountain again."

"Well now, John, digging the Canal is a dangerous job. All the men know that they are taking a great risk. I thought you knew that, too. I understand how you feel, but what are you going to do now in its place?"

"I am going to take a few days and look for some other work. I won't be a burden to you; just give me a few days if you don't mind."

"John, you are my nephew, John Graham's son; you're not going to starve as long as I live. Take all the time you need."

Chapter V: Seeking a New Adventure

And so, for a while, John started hanging around Grant's barbershop, listening to the news that customers brought in with them and their varied opinions about the way things were going with the canal, with politics and the economy both here and back home, and he thought about his dead father who had wanted to see him grow up to be a man like him, and he thought about Uncle Cyrus' words, "You're my nephew, you're a Graham, and as long as I am alive you'll never starve," and of Aunts Sarah and Beulah's words, "So you happy yuh dream a come true to go dig canal with yuh father…" only the dream coming true did not make him happy, it only woke him up to reality, and he thought about the business man on the ship, Mr. Samuel R. Brewster, and he remembered the business card he had given him. It was still in his wallet, and he took it out just to make sure.

"What can I lose," he said to himself, "it is time to seek another kind of adventure."

When Cyrus came home from work that evening, and while they were having supper, John told him about meeting Mr. Samuel R. Brewster on the ship when he was coming to Panama almost a year ago and of the invitation Mr. Brewster had given him to come to Colon and see him about a job.

"At the time, I didn't take it seriously," said John, "but now I think I am going to go and see him."

"If you are sure that's what you want to do, then I wish you the best of luck, son. Let me know how things turn out," Cyrus said to him, and after supper, Cyrus went out for a little while, but John stayed in and tucked in early.

The next morning, he was on the early train heading for Colon, and as he sat in the second-class section collecting his thoughts and taking in the sights along the route, for a moment, the incident of a week ago flashed across his mind, and it only reminded him that he would never go back to digging in the canal again.

As the train pulled into Colon station, there were a lot of people getting off. Apparently, many of them were commuting to work from Panama City as they seemed to be in a hurry. He got off the train and was walking along Front Street looking for the office address written on the card when he saw the sign:

United Fruit Company Travel Agency
&
Employment Office

Samuel R. Brewster, Manager

It was about 9:10 a.m. when a receptionist greeted him as he entered the outer office, and she asked him the purpose of his visit. First, he glanced around and noticed large pictures of United Fruit Company steam ships on the walls, charts with dates and steamship schedules, and in another section, there were pictures of many faraway places, and there were job announcements and titles also on the walls and, on the tables, there were brochures and magazines.

"I am here to see Mr. Samuel R. Brewster," he said, "he asked me to stop in and see him."

"Who shall I say is here to see him?"

"Oh, I am sorry; my name is John Graham, Jr. Tell him we met on the ship coming from Kingston."

"Have a seat, sir, and I will tell Mr. Brewster you are here to see him."

After about five minutes, a medium-height middle-aged gentleman clad in a white Panama suit emerged from the inner office, and he recognized John immediately.

"Hello," said Mr. Brewster, "you're that young man, ah, John Graham, Jr., with the dream of becoming a digger, and you were on your way to meet your dad, right?"

"Yes, I am, or was, when we first met almost a year ago."

"You don't sound so happy about it now. Didn't you meet your father and work on the canal like you said?"

"On both accounts, you see before you now a fatherless son and a disillusioned ex-would-be canal digger."

"Come inside my private office and tell me everything."

And he took John inside his office and gave him a cup of coffee, and John Graham, Jr. told him how he met his uncle Cyrus at the pier instead of his father when he arrived in Colon because his father had suddenly died of a heart attack only two nights earlier while he was at sea on his way to Colon, and how they buried him the next day, how his uncle got him a job in Culebra Cut and while he was working there, just after eight or nine months, he saw a man whom he just had lunch with blown to bits, and he could take it no more, so he quit and he wanted nothing more to do with the canal.

"You know," said Mr. Brewster, "I took to you like my own son when I first saw you on the ship, and I was concerned when you said you wanted to be a digger but to lose your father, that had to be a terrible blow. And then to witness that disaster! That's a lot for a young man like you to take."

"That brings me to the reason I came to see you," said John.

"I think I know why, and I'm certain I can help you, but you will have to travel if you want to take the job."

"As long as I don't have to work near dynamite and landslides!" said John.

"No, nothing like that," said Brewster. "The United Fruit Company is looking to hire workers to work in Cuba on its sugar plantation in Oriente province. I will write a recommendation letter for you to my brother, Carl Brewster, who is a supervisor there and a master carpenter; he will teach you what you need to know and take care of you. I will recommend you for the job as an apprentice carpenter, paying $2 per day, and as you gain experience, you will be promoted to carpenter, earning $3 to $4 per day. The recommendation will include a letter to my brother telling him that you are my stepson. You will be working directly with him in the Central de Oriente. That is the best job for you, pay-wise and labor-wise. You don't want to be a cane cutter in the field; that is too much hard work, and mostly Haitians do that, and it doesn't pay half as much. What do you say? Do you want to take the job?"

"Yes, it is more than I can ask for, and it pays more than the 8 cents an hour the canal pays. But I have one question: why are you being so kind to me?"

"Because you remind me of my son, whom I lost many years ago when he worked for the French. He died in an accident like your friend. He was just like you; he wanted adventure by working in the canal, and it cost him his life."

"How old was your son?"

"He was about your age or a couple of years older when he died in 1889."

"I am sorry to hear that. I hope I don't disappoint you."

"You won't. Remember, the UFC steamer leaves Colon port on Wednesday; that's two days from today. Go home, and get your things, and be back here by 9:15 a.m. on Wednesday. Catch the earliest train from Panama City; I believe it is the 7:30 a.m. train. The ship leaves Colon port at 11:30 a.m., so I'll see you no later than 9:30 a.m. with your passport. I'll have your papers ready when you come."

When he returned home, he told Uncle Cyrus the good news, and Cyrus couldn't be more pleased that this Mr. Brewster would do his nephew such a good turn and had a brother in Cuba to look after him, but he still cautioned John.

"Be careful when you get to Cuba; I hear there may be some trouble in the cities. You're only 18 going on 19; you're not a man yet, and you don't have me over there to look after you (smile.) Write to me as soon as you get there and, in fact, before you go to bed tonight, write your aunts letters. I hope you haven't forgotten about them."

No, he hadn't. In fact, he had written them twice since he got to Panama, once when he learned about his father's death and a few months later when he sent them what he was able to at the time. Now, he is going to have to sugar coat the letter because his aunts may not be pleased with him being alone in Cuba, but what will be will be; he has made his mind up to go no matter what.

He was up early Wednesday morning and bid Uncle Cyrus goodbye, promising to write to him. Uncle Cyrus stuck some bills in his pocket that he was sure he would need and gave him a hug before he walked out the door.

John took the early train as planned and arrived in Colon at about 9:00 a.m. with one piece of luggage and one carry-on bag over his shoulder, both of which contained all of his possessions. With a little effort, he made it to the travel office, and Mr. Brewster was glad he had made it there before 9:30 a.m., as they agreed. There wasn't a lot of time; he had the ticket and the letters ready and papers for him to sign, after which he wanted to go over some of the details, carefully, with John about his travel arrangements.

"Now, I want you to listen carefully," he said, "I have provided you with a ticket to go to Kingston and transfer there to a special UFC transport vessel taking workers to the Banes plantation owned by UFC in Oriente province, Cuba. This letter will introduce you to my brother Carl Brewster, a supervisor at the sugar mill there. Once you reach my brother, he will take care of everything after that. You will not have any time to stop in Kingston to do any visiting; you must board the transport, which leaves immediately after your ship arrives. Now, is everything clear that I have said?"

"At Kingston, how will I know where to go?"

"You just tell them you are transferring to the transport ship to Cuba, you are not stopping in Kingston, and they will direct you to the next ship right there in the harbor for boarding. Once you tell them you are transferring to the transport ship to Cuba, they won't let you go anywhere else but to that ship. And make sure you always have your luggage with you, all right?"

"Yes, everything is clear."

Brewster didn't go into a lengthy explanation. The fact is the UFC was using its fleet of ships to carry workers illegally between the two islands at the time due to their proximity. That is the reason for the caution and indirect transit and transfer instructions.

He then called a cab (horse and buggy) to take them to the pier to clear the port authority for boarding the ship. Mr. Brewster took care of everything, so there was no need to worry; then he shook John's hand and wished him good luck and told him to say hello to his brother for him and send him a post card or letter as soon as he can.

Chapter VI: The Trip to Banes, Cuba, from Kingston

The two-and-a-third-day trip from Panama to Kingston was uneventful, as he had made that same trip in the other direction only a year ago, and nothing had changed. It was at Kingston when he went through the transfer procedure and boarded the U.F.C. transport ship that he found himself among a mass of workers like himself going to Cuba to work as cane cutters, grass cutters, railway workers, sugar mill workers, boiler workers, carpenters, store clerks, stock clerks, sales clerks and cooks that he realized how massive the sugar business in Cuba must be. Many of the men on board were Jamaicans and were experienced craftsmen, and many had already worked in the sugar industry in Jamaica. In general, most foreign workers who went to Cuba were Haitians who did the job of cutting cane.

The trip from Kingston port to Antilla port in Cuba took almost 19 hours or a little less than one day. Since they left Kingston at about 7 p.m. Friday, October 27, 1911, they arrived at Antilla around 2 p.m. Saturday, October 28, 1911, a few days before the harvest season or Zafra was scheduled to begin. That time of the year, from November to April (the dry season in Cuba), the heavy work of harvesting the cane was done. At that time, too, most of the labor force was brought in to do the cutting, bundling, loading, and moving of the cane stalks to the sugar mills, where the cane was converted into sugar and molasses.

At the harbor port, the new arrivals were all processed by UFC as well as by local harbor personnel and taken by surface transportation to the Banes sugar plantation in northeastern Oriente, Cuba, to be settled and housed, and prepared for their assignments to do the heavy work that is to be done.

The following day after John arrived, he met his newly adopted uncle, Carl Brewster, to whom he gave the letter of introduction from Carl's brother, Samuel. Carl read the letter, then sized up John Graham Jr. and, after a few seconds, spoke.

"My brother seems to think highly of you, to make you his stepson. Tell me about yourself, your age, where you come from, your background, what you know, and there's only one thing I insist on always, that is honesty, so tell me the truth no matter what."

This was tough for John because he didn't know where to begin, whether to tell the truth or lie a little bit, but judging from the look on his make-believe uncle's face, he knew if he made anything up, he would see through him in a minute.

"My name is John Graham, Jr. I will be 19 next February; I was born in Trench Pen, St. Andrew, Jamaica, and both of my parents are dead. I have two aunts in Kingston named Sarah and Beulah Graham. My father, John Graham, Sr., was a master carpenter for the Panama Canal when he suddenly had a heart attack and died when I was on my way to him in Panama. His brother, Cyrus Graham, who lived with my father, came to meet me when I arrived in Colon and took me to live with him in Panama City. From there, he got me a job on the Panama Canal as a pinche at the excavation site. There, I saw a man blown to bits by dynamite in Culebra Cut, and I told my uncle Cyrus Graham I didn't want to work for the canal anymore. That's when I went to your brother, whom I had met on the boat when I was going to Panama to meet my father, and he said I reminded him of his son, who was also killed in the canal. I am not really his stepson; he just felt sorry for me, I guess, and was trying to help me get a job."

Carl looked at him again carefully and shook his head, then asked him a curious question.

"Did you say your father's name is John Graham, Sr., originally from St. Andrew, Jamaica?

"Yes, sir."

"And your uncle's name is Cyrus Graham?"

"Yes, sir."

"I am glad you told the truth, son because I want you to know something. Your father and I and your uncle Cyrus were very good friends when we were little boys playing in Trench Pen yard a long time ago. Your father was left-handed and had a nickname, "magga foot," when he was a boy because he was skinny. I knew your family, and I knew your grandfather, too. He was one of the best carpenters in Kingston, and it's he who taught me and your father carpentry. Boy, come here. You are not only honest, but you are like family to me. You don't have to worry about anything."

"I don't know what to say, but I am grateful to you and your brother," said John.

"No, be grateful to your father, John Graham, Sr. Is he looking out for you from beyond who makes you come to the right people, his people. Look here now: if they give you quarters in the "barracones" on the plantation, tell them you don't want it. You are coming and living right here with me and my wife Estelle, you hear me."

And that is how John Graham was introduced to Cuba that day on the Banes plantation in the province of Oriente. He moved in with Carl and his wife Estelle, who had a home in Pueblo Nuevo, a neighborhood in the plantation town where only Jamaicans lived. Carl made sure he was signed on as an assistant carpenter working directly with him.

One day at dinner, they were conversing.

"So, you are John Graham's son," said Estelle. "I was a little girl in Trench Pen, too, when we were all little children together, your father, Cyrus, Carl, and me. That's how Carl and I met, and when we grew up, we came here to Cuba. It's not so bad here, but one day, we hope to go back home. Tell me about your aunties and your grandmother if she is still alive; she was one kind person and could cook for days."

"I don't remember granny too well because she died when I was a baby, but Aunt Sarah and Aunt Beulah still live in the house my grandfather built, and after my father left Jamaica to join his brother Cyrus in Panama and work on the Panama Canal, my aunts took care of me until he sent for me.

After my father passed away in Panama, I stayed there with my uncle Cyrus Graham until Samuel Brewster got me this job in Cuba."

"When you write home, give Carl's and my regards to your aunts and let them know how sorry we are about their brother's passing. They will remember me and Carl, I am sure," said Estelle.

"In the letter, my brother wrote me," added Carl, "he tells me you used to be handy around the house in Trench Pen. Tell me what you know so I have an idea before I put you to work."

"When I was a little boy before daddy left for Panama, he bought me a little carpenter set, and he used to show me how to use the hammer and saw. I loved to play with them a lot, and when I grew older, I would fix things around the house and in the neighbors' houses."

"I guess it must be in your blood then, handed down from grandfather to son to grandson. I'll make a master carpenter out of you yet."

Chapter VII: Settling Down on the Banes Plantation

It was now the first week in November 1912, the beginning of the Zafra (cane harvesting) season, and the plantation was bustling with workers, and there was much work to be done. Early in the morning, the workers were out in the field, and the cane cutting began from morning till noon till late evening. It was hard work to meet the goal of producing 7.5 tons of raw sugar in one season since that would require harvesting over 161 million pounds of sugar cane. One can understand why the United Fruit Company planted more than 330,000 acres of cane on their plantation, which would require thousands of workers working 6 months a year from November to April to harvest. It also shows how profitable that industry is when sugar is sold at $0.50 a pound, and the price would even go higher from time to time. Labor was cheap, especially since the majority of workers were cutters and laborers who made between $0.40 and $1.00 per day. Higher-paid workers (managers, overseers, accountants, carpenters, train conductors, drivers, mechanics, bricklayers, cooks) were in the minority and made between $2.00 to $5.00 per day. One can only imagine that as production increased, so did the profits and the richer and richer the owners became.

So much for economics, John Graham didn't do so badly for himself, either, for, as an assistant carpenter, his wages in Cuba were $2.00 per day, much more than he was paid as a pinche on the canal ($0.08 per hour.) Work was hard, but at least he didn't have to stay all day out in the hot sun cutting grass or cane; he worked mostly in the mill house with his adopted uncle Carl, except sometimes when they were required to do carpentry work outdoors. He was fortunate. He was settled; he had a job and a place to live with Carl and Estelle, who turned out to be more than just strangers in a strange country. He was curious, though, because certain questions lingered in his mind. One evening, while they were having dinner, he tried to get some answers.

"Uncle Carl, do you mind if I call you uncle?"

"Of course not," said Carl, "we are almost like family anyway; I don't mind that at all."

"I want to know more about the way people live in this country, especially on the plantation, and what they do besides work in the cane fields and the mill?"

"I am happy to tell you everything I know, and what I don't know, I'll find out for you. About the country, I don't know too much, except most Cubans are descended from the large slave population the Spaniards brought to the island centuries ago before emancipation, and they consider themselves Cubans. Not many Cubans work on the plantation because, in general, they frown on plantation work, but some do, as you probably have already found out. This is a big island, and Estelle and I hardly travel outside the plantation. Right now, I don't think African Cubans are so happy about the way the white Cubans are treating them, but that's none of my concern, or yours if we stay here and don't get involved. This here is the Banes sugar cane plantation, owned by the United Fruit Company, which owns a lot of land in this part of Cuba for growing sugar cane to make sugar and molasses. They built massive sugar mills, miles and miles of railroad lines, hospitals, shipping ports, electric plants, water treatment facilities, firehouses, warehouses, bakeries, commissaries, and dairies. Bringing so many immigrants from abroad from places like Haiti, Jamaica, other Caribbean islands, and Central America, the population of immigrant workers in Banes is very large.

To accommodate so many workers and their families, they built towns (racially segregated) that are complete with all the facilities needed for living. It has houses for families, as well as quarters (barracoons) for bachelors, and is equipped with everything, including primary schools, churches, an exclusive club, stores, restaurants, cafés, recreation centers, and even a pastoral home and/or a temple. In the Jamaican neighborhood, called Pueblo Nuevo or Jamaica Town, in addition to everything else, we have a cricket field as well."

"But Uncle Carl, if the workers work such long hours each day, when have they any time for recreation?"

"Maybe they don't have much time during the Zafra or harvest season from November to April because the workdays are long, usually 10 hours or more, but the workers have Sundays off and one or two holidays when they can relax. Sometimes, they gather in the cafés in the recreation center or in each other's dwelling place to socialize. Most of the workers you see around the plantation are seasonal workers, and they look forward to extended relaxation time and fun during the "Tiempo muerto," or rainy season when the Zafra is finished, and work slackens off in the months of May through October. Those workers with higher level skills, such as tailors, watchmakers, cobblers, barbers, shopkeepers, artisans, mechanics, cooks, etc., do not have to depend solely on the "Zafra" to make a living and so have less trouble finding employment in the "Tiempo muerto." Many of the seasonal workers, however, either go back to their countries after "Zafra," or, if they choose to stay on the plantation, they remain idle, or they turn to creative forms of earning income such as gambling, selling clandestine lottery, selling trinkets and odds and ends, you name it. Some even go into the business of procuring madams of questionable repute from the cities and bringing them onto the plantation to accommodate lonely bachelors in the cafes. As I said previously, not many Cubans work on the plantation, but those who do usually go back to their Cuban cities and villages after the Zafra season is over. It is my advice to you that you always stay here on the plantation because it is separated from the larger Cuban towns and cities where it is not safe. I hope I answered all your questions, son. Is there anything else you want to know?"

"No, not for right now; thank you, you have given me plenty of information."

It was well into the year 1912 and approaching the end of Zafra. John was settled in his job on the plantation by this time, and he wasted no time writing to Samuel Brewster to thank him and tell him how well things were going for him in Cuba. He also wrote to his uncle and aunts to give them Carl and Estelle's regards and address so that they could communicate since they turned out to be childhood friends.

He got to know a few of the workers in the mill and around the plantation and soon became friends with Julio Ramos, who was a boiler specialist; Pedro Augustin, a railway worker; Juan Linares, a warehouse worker; and Francis Warner, a restaurant worker, and an excellent tailor. All of them, except for Francis Warner and himself, happened to be Afro-Cubans. Francis was from Jamaica, and he came to Banes a year before John did.

One Saturday afternoon near the end of April 1912, as he was leaving the mill, Julio called out to him.

"Hey, John Graham, what are you doing this evening? Want to stop and have a beer at Mirabella?" He was with Pedro as they were leaving work together.

John thought about it for a second, and at that moment in his mind, he convinced himself that he had grown tired and bored by now of going to the plantation theatre in his spare time to see silent movies. He had seen Custer's Last Fight, Homer's Odyssey, and From the Manger to the Cross many times, but now he wished for another diversion. In Panama, his uncle Cyrus had told him he was not old enough to be seen in a cantina; however, this was Cuba, and he was 19 years old now and could pass for 21. Besides, who would know the difference here on the plantation? So, he replied to Juan.

"Yes, of course, I'll meet you there later."

Later that evening, both he and Francis went to the Mirabella bar to meet Julio, Pedro, and Juan. There, they met other Cubans, Haitians, and Jamaicans, drinking Cuban beer, Cuban rum, and Jamaican rum. While they were enjoying themselves, they could hear on the radio what sounded like news and political propaganda. It was coming directly from Havana, the capital of Cuba, which is farther west of Banes and which is the largest city in Cuba. On the radio, they were talking about some new law called the Morua law that banned Afro-Cubans from organizing political parties or running for political office. It was soon apparent that all the Afro-Cubans, especially Julio, Perez, and Juan, were against this law and gave their support to the PIC organization (The Partido Independiente de Color – an Afro-Cuban organization fighting to have the Morua law that was adopted on Feb. 14, 1910, repealed.)

"Ya los amantes de los Yanquis han Ganado otra vez. Estan en contra con el espiritu de marti y Maceo. Que paso con los gritos de los guerreros y patriotas de la Guerra de independencia? Que paso con Cuba libre, con la lucha para derechos e igualdad para todos los Cubanos?" cried out one of the staunch PIC supporters sitting in the bar.

Julio turned to the others to see what their reaction was.

"Maybe he shouldn't shout so loud. You never know who is listening. I don't trust anyone in this pro-Yankee government," said Juan.

"My father is a member of the Partido Independiente de Color," said Pedro Augustin, "and all over Oriente province, they are mobilizing people everywhere to support them and to stand up for equal rights and opportunities for all Cubans, white and black."

"Why are you Cubans always fighting with each other?" asked Francis.

"You should know," said Julio, "look what the British did to your country during and after slavery. After slavery here in Cuba and after the Spaniards were driven out, it was the gringos who came and brought racial hatred back into our country and turned the whites against the blacks. They are trying to make Cuba "white," but it will never work."

"I don't understand," said John, "don't you have a democratic form of government and a constitution in Cuba?"

"John, you are so naïve; you live cooped up on the plantation, but there's a whole world outside the plantations that you know nothing about. The masses of Cuban people have been struggling for a very long time under oppressive powers, and countless numbers of them have given their lives for freedom. For twenty years, we have fought Spain for independence and the right to live in a free and fair society, and now that we have won our independence, should we be enslaved again?"

"What about your Cuban government, aren't they there to defend the people against unjust treatment?"

"What government?" uttered Julio, "you mean a puppet government made up of traitors who have sold their country out to the Americans and who would rather see Cuban People under an American slave master that is no different than the one we got rid of? John, you need to go and visit Camaguey, Cienfuegos, Manzanillo, Songo, La Maya, Boqueron, Las Tunas, Guantanamo, Bayamo, Holquin, Santiago de Cuba, and Havana to see what is going on and to meet the real Cuban people, and you will understand. When I leave here after the Zafra is over, I am going back to join my people in La Maya township and stand with the PIC. If you got a taste for adventure like you say, and if you want to learn something about us Afro-Cubans whose ancestors, like yours in Jamaica, came from Africa as slaves, then I invite you to come with me to my hometown and meet my people."

"I would like very much to come if I can get the time off in May."

"That shouldn't be a problem for you; I'm sure you have some vacation time coming to you as an annual worker, and La Maya is not too far from here; it's only a few hours south from here to Santiago de Cuba."

"I am from La Maya, too," said Juan, "so count me in."

"I am from a little town called Yateras in Guantanamo province," said Pedro. "We are all from the southeast Oriente region, which includes Santiago de Cuba. Most of the population there are Afro-Cubans."

Francis, so as not to be left out, said he would join the group.

"At least John would have company when he returns to Banes," added Francis.

Chapter VIII: The Trip to La Maya and its Aftermath

So, it was agreed that the four of them would travel together to La Maya after the Zafra harvest ended in early May 1912. Carl and Estelle didn't think it was a good idea for him to go, but he was determined and said he wanted to see another part of the island and learn more about the Afro-Cuban people. So, on May 18, 1912, the group left Banes together, heading towards La Maya by train. Pedro Augustin, a train operator on the Cuban Company Railway, knows all the routes and every interconnection of the railway lines, so it wasn't hard for him to figure out a way they could take the train from Banes and after a few stops and connections it would bring them to La Maya in about 2 to 4 hours. La Maya was one of the stops on the train that was going toward Guantanamo, Cuba. There were five stops: Queto, Alto Cedro, Julia Melia, San Luis, and La Maya, including two transfer points, one at Queto and one at San Luis. It would be roughing it a little bit, but they had the fortitude and patience that it took to get them to their destination and back.

About 4 hours later, they arrived in the village of La Maya, tired and a little exhausted from the journey. They stopped by Julio's home, where they were warmly greeted and offered a welcome meal.

"Companeros, this is my family. "Les presento a mi papa, Francisco Ramos; mi mama, Gloria Ramos; y mi hermana, Maria Ramos."

"Bienvenidos! Bienvenidos a todos," responded his parents.

"Mama y papa permitenme presentarles a mes amigos de trabajo. Juan Linares es de aqui mismo; Pedro Augustin es de Yateras en Guantanamo; y los otros dos, John Graham y Francis Warner, son Jamaicanos. John y Francis no hablan mucho espanol y, si se pueden, por favor, les hablan en ingles."

"No problem," responded Julio's father, who is a native Afro-Cuban, "I speak a little English, which I picked up from your mother and from my Jamaican friends; what I don't know, you will help me with, Julio. Tell them not to worry."

"My parents were bi-lingual," said Julio's mother, Gloria Ramos, "they were born in Jamaica; I came here with them when I was a little girl, so English is not a problem for me."

"I speak a little English, too," said Maria, Julio's sister, who was also there to greet them when they arrived.

Julio's father was a Guerrero in the mambi army that fought against the Spanish, and his mother, who has maroon blood in her, is a staunch supporter and would gladly take up arms at his side if she had to; and his sister, Maria, she thinks she is a little Guerrera, too, at least in spirit.

Somehow, the conversation over dinner went well in both languages, with a lot of goodwill and laughter. Julio's father brought them up to date on local events and politics, which Julio was very much interested in since he had left almost a year ago to go to Banes to work, just before the Zafra season, and much had been taking place in his absence.

"What about the struggle for the rights of all Cubans and the repeal of that monstrous law?" Julio asked his dad.

"We will talk about that later, Julio; right now, let's enjoy your homecoming, and let's taste some wine and eat some of your mother's good cooking while we get to know your friends better."

That's when his father, Francisco Ramos, found out that Pedro Augustin's father, Antonio Augustin, had also served in the Mambises, like himself, during the war for independence.
"Your father and I served under el Titano de Bronze during the war. How we loved that man, Maceo, and didn't fear the Spaniards who outnumbered us 10 to 1. We fought like tigers under his brilliant command. Tell your father hello for me when you get home, and please don't forget."

"He was wounded in the last battle near Soledad; I don't know if you knew that."

"No, I didn't. Our units got separated at one time, and I didn't catch up with him. Was he badly wounded?"

"He took a bullet in his leg, and he still has a slight limp from it; otherwise, he will tell you he is fine compared to the enemies he killed. He's kind of proud, you know."

"I can imagine. We drank a few "copas" together on one or two occasions. He is a fine man with a good sense of humor, I remember."

"And dad," said Julio, "I think you should know Juan's father, too, Joaquin Linares; he is from the barrio Ti Arriba, which is not far from here."

"I know where it is," said his father, "and I know Joaquin Linares. He is a veteran just like Antonio Augustin and me. A lot of veterans settled here in La Maya after the war. Como esta la familia, Juan?" asked Francisco.

"Estan muy bien senor Ramos. Mi papa tambien esta orgulloso de su servicio militar bajo el mando del general Maceo. Habla de eso todo el tiempo."

"Si, como todos los veteranos. Saludelo a su padre para mi cuando lo ve."

And from time to time, the conversation switched back and forth from English to Spanish and vice versa.

Julio's dad noticed John sitting quietly next to Maria and said to Julio:

"Julio, why don't you properly introduce your sister to your Jamaican friend?"

"He seems to have done that already, dad." Turning to John and Maria, Julio said slyly, "For someone who doesn't speak Spanish and someone who doesn't speak English too well, you two seem to be getting along okay."

"Don't worry about us," said John, "If we don't know the words, we can always use sign language. Isn't that right, Maria?"

"Of course, we'll manage," said Maria.

What Julio and his father didn't know was that ever since he arrived, John had his eyes on Maria, who was receptive and equally attracted to him. She has beautiful skin, not jet black but of a darkish shade. She is of medium height and has lovely hair, which she wears in two braids parted in the middle and pinned behind both ears. She has a beautiful smile and looks so pretty whenever she smiles. She wore a short skirt which revealed her neatly shaped legs that he had not failed to notice.

After dinner, Juan and Pedro said their despedidas, Pedro heading for Yateras, Guantanamo, and Juan for a nearby finca in Ti Arriba. John and Francis, however, remained guests at Ramos' home.

It was nearing sunset as Mr. Ramos, Julio, and Francis sat on the front porch of the Ramos' modest home, drinking berry juice and an occasional shot of Cuban rum made from molasses in one of the nearby rum plants. The Ramos had a small piece of land on which they grew cassava, yams, potatoes, mangoes, plantain, and some vegetables and raised a few chickens; however, for half of the year, Francisco Ramos did seasonal work in the coffee plantation near Sierra Maestra mountains a few miles south from where he lives. He is a little better off than most Afro-Cuban veterans and Cubans of color who have been marginalized by the pro-white, pro-Yankee government running the country. But he still doesn't feel secure and doesn't know when he may be a victim of the government that has been forcefully taking their lands away to sell to these big sugar companies and to foreign land grabbers.

"I didn't want to mention this during dinner, but the politics is heating up more and more every day," he said to Julio and Francis as they sat together on the porch after dinner.

John and Maria had strolled a short distance from the house and were sitting on a tree stump, enjoying each other's company.

"Why did they name this town La Maya?" asked John, "I thought that Mayans were Indians from Mexico?"

"No, the name has nothing to do with Mexico," replied Maria, "notice that there is a long stretch of giant trees for a good distance around the outskirts of the town. Those trees are called maya or ceiba trees, and they were planted there to protect the people in this area; the Africans believed that these trees have mystical, spiritual powers. Therefore, the town got its name, la Maya (town of the Maya trees)."

"That's very interesting," said John, "what else is there about this country that I should know?"

"Well, for another thing, if you travel about 50 miles west, you will come to the town of Yara near Manzanillo where in 1512, the Taino chief Hatuey, the first Cuban revolutionary in history, was bound to a tamarind tree and burned alive by the Spaniards; and if you go half that distance west of here you'll be in the town of Baire where on 2-24-1895 the final war of independence began and near there is the little town of Dos Rios where Jose Marti was killed in battle in 1895 fighting for independence; also, less than a mile west of here, is the town of Majaguabo, San Luis which is the birthplace of the great general Antonio Maceo, hero of the revolutionary war; and if you go east in the opposite direction you will come to Yateras, Guantanamo where your friend Pedro Augustin lives and where south of there the Americans occupy Guantanamo Bay, the easternmost part of Cuba. Just a short distance from where we are standing now if you go south, you will come to the first capital of Cuba, Santiago de Cuba, and, if you were to visit us in June and July and go to Santiago de Cuba, you would see the biggest and most spectacular carnival in all of Cuba that is celebrated there every year."

"Carnival… I thought carnival was celebrated in February, just before Lent?" said John.

"In Santiago de Cuba, it's a little different. We call our carnival "mamarrachos," and we celebrate it on our patron saints' days: St. John (6/24), St. Peter (6/29), St. Christine (7/24), St. James (7/25), and St. Anne (7/26) to show our thanks for the harvest season or Zafra."

"Then you don't observe Lent and celebrate Easter here in Cuba?"

"Sure, we do, but not with a carnival to chase away evil spirits. We go to church. All that excitement and boisterous celebrations we do during the mamarrachos."

"You mean parades and so on?"

"Yes, with music, dancing, drinking, carousing, wearing of costumes and masks, etc. We also have bonfires at night and pilgrimages to sanctuaries carrying torches in our hands. And there are tables spread with food, drinks, and fruits for sale, and, of course, on the last day, 7/29, a grand parade takes place. Everybody goes to Santiago to party during the days of mamarrachos."

"If I can, I will certainly come back again in July to go to your carnival with you. Would you like that?"

"Yes, and I guarantee you will have a good time."

In the meantime, back on the porch, the conversation with Julio, Julio's father, and his friend Francis continued to center on Cuban politics.

"What do you mean heating up?" asked Julio.

"I mean, the leaders of the Partido Independiente de Color are calling for demonstrations in all the provinces to mobilize for the November elections, and they are planning to have huge gatherings in various parts of Oriente soon. Some of the PIC leaders are going to speak to the people to rally support for their movement against unjust treatment and for equal rights."

"When will this take place?" asked Julio.

"I was told that the biggest open-air gathering is set for the 20th in the village of Jamaica, Guantanamo."

"That would mean the day after tomorrow, Monday, May 20, 1912?"

"Yes, and every Cuban of color should attend."

"Let's go to that one," said Julio, "it is near where Pedro lives; I am sure we will see him there."

"You young folks should go; your mother and I will stay here and keep an eye on the farm. Take Maria along with you, too."

On the day of the gathering in Jamaica, the village square was crowded to capacity, and, just as they thought, they were lucky to run into Pedro and his father. You could sense the feeling of urgency and excitement as the crowds quieted down, and the program began with the introduction of the representatives of the Partido Independiente de Color. The first speaker was the co-leader of PIC, Evaristo Estenoz, who was also a founder and a former general in the Mambi army that fought alongside Antonio Maceo in the war of independence against Spain.

"Greetings to you, my brothers and sisters… Viva Cuba libre!! Viva la revolucion!!" were his first words, which got a loud, emotional response, *"Viva Cuba libre!! Viva la revolucion!!"* then the speaker continued (in Spanish), *"As you know, our great leader Jose Marti, the father of the Cuban Revolution against Spain, believed in a free Cuba for all. In 1895, he published the Montecristi Manifesto, in which he proclaimed that the republic should be just and fair for all and for the wellbeing of all people without distinction of race, sex, or social position. He proclaimed that on the shoulders of Afro-Cubans. Cuba is going to win its independence, and when that victory is won, the republic must serve all Cubans equally, whether white, black, or mulatto.*

As a matter of fact, ninety percent of the Cuban revolutionary army was Afro-Cuban, and of the 108,000 Cubans who died in the war, 82,000 of them were Afro-Cubans. Our people gave their lives for this republic, believing that they would be treated equally and fairly when the war was over. That is what Marti and Maceo had promised. That is what we fought for. But when it appeared certain that the Black Mambises Cuban army was going to win the war and have a voice in government, the white plantocracy called in and allied themselves with the Americans, who then intervened and virtually took over Cuba by force and set up a pro-white, pro-U.S. puppet government that then resolved to wage a "Guerrita de Raza," (Race War) Purging Blacks in Cuba and returning us back to quasi slave status. The first thing they did was to demobilize the Liberation Army, annul all the gains made by Afro-Cubans, including political positions, military ranks, and public offices held by thousands of blacks, and, to add insult to injury, the puppet government under treacherous Jose Miguel Gomez instituted a new law, the Morua Law of

1909 which took away the rights of all Afro-Cubans to participate in the political process. They would not let us have a voice in either the Liberal Party or the Conservative Party, and that is the reason we were left with no alternative but to form our own party, the (PIC) Partido Independiente de Color to overturn the unjust Morua law, to strive to represent our people and to improve conditions for all Cuban citizens disenfranchised and marginalized because of their color.

To show the world what we stand for collectively, we call your attention to the following objectives and goals as written in the PIC publication "Prevision." We aim for nothing less than to achieve these goals:

- *The end of Morua law.*
- *Repatriation at the government expense of every Cuban wishing to return to their country of origin if they cannot afford it on their own.*
- *The end of racial discrimination in all sectors of the republic.*
- *Distribution of government lands to landless citizens and a review of those acquired during U. S. military intervention.*
- *Equal access to education and government jobs for all Cubans.*
- *The end to a ban on non-white immigration.*
- *End of selective immigration for the purpose of making Cuba white.*
- *Compulsory free education for all Cubans 8-14 years of age.*
- *Establishment of an 8-hour workday.*
- *Establishment of a law against child labor.*
- *Insurance against accidents in the workplace.*
- *Appointment of citizens of color to the diplomatic service body.*
- *Prison reform with the purpose of rehabilitating and retraining inmates prior to reintegrating them into society.*

- *Establishment of trial by jury of one's peers.*
- *Abolition of the death penalty.*

The Partido Independiente de Color does not aspire for black supremacy any more than for white supremacy and regards all blacks and whites as equals under the laws of God and men in a free society.

What we are fighting for is just and no more than we have a right to, as Cuban citizens and as human beings. We were willing to lay down our lives for the independence of this new republic, and it is only fair that this republic should grant us our rights in return. We are willing to use the ballot and the pen to seek those rights, but if necessary, we will stick together, and we will defend our rights as aggrieved citizens.

Down with Morua law!! Viva Cuba libre!! Viva la revolucion!!" he shouted.

And those words were followed by the crowd echoing back the Grito:

"Down with Morua law!! Viva Cuba Libre!! Viva la revolucion!!"

Throughout Oriente and Santa Clara provinces, similar meetings and demonstrations were taking place while they were demonstrating in Jamaica Guantanamo. After demonstrations in the village of Jamaica that evening, the group stopped in a local cantina in Yateras to have some refreshments and a discussion with Pedro and some friends while the inspired words of Gen. Estenoz and the fervor of the occasion were still stirring within them; but, before they parted, Pedro made a very wise and ominous observation.

"Things are going to get a little rough here in Oriente in the coming weeks," said Pedro. "You don't know what these people are capable of. If it was bad before, it will get worse now. I fear open hostility is coming. I believe you, John, and Francis, since you don't live here, you should be thinking about returning to Banes soon. How long did you plan to stay, anyway?"

"We had planned to stay for about two weeks originally. That would mean up until about June 1st or 2nd," said John.

"I must go back to Banes myself since I left my wife and two children there. I had planned to stay two weeks and had left them there where I believed they would be safe. I am anxious now to get back to them, so if you want to go back with me, I am leaving on Wednesday, May 23rd. I'll pass by the Ramos' place and pick you up if you want to go."

Until he heard the urgency in Pedro's voice, he had not appreciated that there was any danger, but Pedro is from these parts, and he must know what he is talking about.

"Okay with me. Is that okay with you, Francis?"

"Yes," said Francis, "I would hate to get caught down here in some kind of race war. I'll be ready to go back with you whenever you are."

After that exciting day and a pleasant evening in Yateras, they parted and headed back for La Maya. It was a little late when they arrived, and Mr. Ramos didn't hesitate to tell them what he had heard on the radio coming from Havana and the western region. The whites now had the excuse they had always wanted. All day and night, they ranted and swore about how evil black people were, that the Blacks were raping white women. The whites were being stirred up by the white media; enemies of PIC exploited the opportunity to arouse in them the fear of blacks rising and taking over; militias were formed; Jose Miguel Gomez, head of the white government of Cuba, dispatched the army into Oriente with the mission to "search and destroy the PIC and their sympathizers." The next day and the days following were the same thing, only worse; they were attacking black Cubans, and the U.S. was threatening to take over if the Cuban government didn't do something to stabilize the country. Under the circumstances, Ramos agreed that John and Francis should leave La Maya immediately for their own safety. Julio and Maria were determined to stay with their parents and do what they could to safeguard their property and themselves.

Early the next morning, Wednesday, May 23, Pedro came to get John and Francis, and they took off for the north shore heading towards Banes, hoping that their only hardship would be some delays, perhaps, on the trains going back. The La Maya train stop was not far from where they were, but from there, everything would be uncertain, the way things were stirring up all over the island. Luckily, they didn't have to wait too long for a train heading back to San Luis and then north to the Cueto en route to the last stop, Banes. The problem was when they approached Cueto, Pedro got news from other railway workers that there was danger going north toward Banes because most of Oriente Province and even the highways and trains were not safe where they were heading. Militias and Cuban soldiers were all about and were boarding the trains, especially in the northern and eastern regions, looking for PIC members, sympathizers, and anyone who was a dark-skinned Cuban to kill them, and it didn't make any difference. As they pulled into the Cueto station, they could see up ahead a formation of white-armed militiamen waiting for the train as it approached. They started to feel the terror from thinking of the fate that awaited them.

"Pedro, what are we going to do? What are we going to do?" pleaded Francis.

"We are not getting off the train; maybe they're just checking people who are getting off, and they'll just let us through."

But no such luck! Six heavily armed militias boarded the train and started pointing out their suspected victims, including Pedro, John, Francis, and a half dozen other Afro-Cubans on the train. Somewhere between Baguanos and Banes, they made the conductor stop the train and forced their human quarry off with them, U.S. western cowboy style, before allowing the train to continue. At gunpoint, they goaded them into the woodland area
, apparently with evil intent. While they were going through the woods, one of the other six frightened victims must have

panicked, tripped, and fallen, and the villains pounced with their rifles pointed straight at him.

"Levantate! Levantate! O si muere aqui o mas tarde, no importa! Levantate!"

I do not know where bravery comes from, but this is where Pedro, Francis, and John decided to make a break for it, live or die, for if they did nothing, it would be certain death by firing squad. They loosened their ropes and dashed off, each in a different direction in a do-or-die attempt. All ten captives ran as the bullets began to fly; they couldn't kill them all at the same time.

In their desperation to escape the mob, who had deadly weapons and murderous intent, Pedro, John, and Francis got separated; John and Francis went in one direction and Pedro in another, with at least a half dozen pursuers shooting at them. John and Francis ended up on the beach near Playa Blanca with the sea in front of them and the murderous militia behind them. Only the sea offered an escape. Fortunately, some fisherman had anchored his boat on the shore near the edge of the water, and they frantically dragged it into the sea and tried to paddle as hurriedly as they could away from the shore as the rifles kept firing at them from the beach. It was at that moment, he recalled that his friend Francis had stood up in a foolish attempt to hurl curses at the militia squad when he was fatally shot and fell overboard. He died instantly and sank below the surface. John kept on rowing until he was finally out of the range of fire. He was safe from the militia at last, he thought, but his good friend was gone, and he was alone, adrift, and exposed to the treacherous waters of the Atlantic Ocean.

Chapter IX: Three Frantic Days on the Atlantic
(May 23 – 25, 1912)

The hours went by very slowly. Soon, the shores had disappeared, and there was no land in sight. Shielding himself from the rays of the sun as best as he could with a piece of canvas found in the boat, he had given up paddling, which seemed to serve no purpose except to use up his strength. The sun started to go down, and it was getting darker. There was nothing in sight, only the vast sea, the sky above, and the approaching darkness. He could smell and feel the ocean all around him and hear its silence like the stillness of eternity. He never knew how desolate the sea could be, how deathly the silence, and how frightful the desperation that creeps into the heart and soul when one is faced with the prospect of imminent and inevitable extinction.

It would only take one angry wave, one raging swell, to write the end; that's only a matter of time before the biding sea should decide or his endurance should give way. He wanted to cry. Is this the way his life was going to end? If it were to end here, it was such a short one; he had not even reached his 20th birthday. How would his uncle Cyrus back in Caledonia and his aunts Sarah and Beulah in Kingston take the news if the worst happened? Will they blame themselves in some way? Even now, they must be thinking about him and wondering if and when they will ever hear from him or see him again. He also thought about Carl and Estelle Brewster, with whom he had been living during the past year in Banes, Cuba. They must be worried to death right now, wondering if he is ever coming back to Banes again. If only he had stayed on the plantation as Carl and Estelle had advised him to do. If only he had not gone to La Maya that day. It did no good now to have regrets; it was too late for that. He looked up at the stars in the heavens and prayed for a miracle. Soon, he dosed off, and when he opened his eyes, it was daylight again, and he had drifted farther and farther out to sea. Nothing but sea and sky all around, and nothing he could do but hope and pray. He tried his best to keep from panicking as the day kept creeping along and the boat kept drifting further and further, and he could not keep his mind from wandering, as in a daydream, and he started to recall the events of the past two years in his life that led him to where he now finds himself.

He had been daydreaming for how long, he did not know, when, suddenly, he was returned to reality by a few waves splashing against and over the boat, causing it to sway from side to side before it calmed itself again. No, this was not the fatal wave, not yet, he thought, and hoped the sea would be his friend. It was now approaching evening again. He could tell by the sun's oblique rays and the shadow made in the boat, and the heat was not so intense. Then, he began to imagine that he heard his father's voice speaking to him.

"Just keep holding on, son, and keep praying. You know yesterday you had no choice; it was either death by the militia or taking your chances with the sea. At least you are still alive. Pray, my son, miracles do happen, you know."

Maybe he gained strength from the hallucination, but it was only the second day. How long, he thought, at this rate could he last? He had heard that a man could go without food for three weeks and without water for three days. Those facts were no consolation, though, as he prepared to deal once more with the darkness, the lonely night, and with his fears. The waters, which were somewhat calmer, kept lapping at the sides of the boat as if the lips of the ocean were savoring their next victim. No, he chided himself, stop thinking such thoughts; maybe tomorrow help will come. And soon, after several more hours, he dosed off and fell asleep again.

When he opened his eyes, it was daylight once more, and he had drifted farther out to sea. It was the third day adrift on the Atlantic Ocean, and he dreaded the prospect of another day without food or water. The sun was going down again, and soon, another day would be gone. It was going to be three days, and he did not believe he could last another day as thirst and hunger pangs now gripped angrily at his stomach. With no provisions and no sense of direction, and at the mercy of the elements, he was almost ready to resign himself to his fate, and when it seemed that all hope was about to fail him, his miracle appeared in the form of a dim shape at first in the distance. It got closer, and then he realized that it was not a figment of his imagination but a real ocean steamer that had suddenly come out of nowhere. It was now within a fraction of a mile and was getting even closer; then, it was only several hundred yards away. All the while, he did not realize how frantically and how desperately he had been waving at it, and they must have seen his signal as they approached his little craft. He had taken off his shirt and had waved it in the air till he almost toppled the boat in his desperate efforts. This was fate, he thought; fate was on his side, after all, as it seemed his life would now be spared.

Chapter X: Rescued by the S.S. Bayano
(May 25, 1912)

It wasn't long before he was on board the steamer, wetting his thirst and tasting a warm meal, after which he was questioned by the captain.

"What in hell were you doing out there on the Atlantic Ocean all alone in that little craft?" asked the captain. "You know the chances of your survival if we hadn't come along when we did? You must live a charmed life. I know you have to have a damn good story to tell."

"Yes, I do," said John, and he began to relate to the captain the events that led up to the moment he was rescued:

"I left Panama eight months ago and went to Cuba, where I lived and worked in the sugar mill on the Banes plantation. After the sugar harvest ended in May, I was visiting some of my Cuban friends in La Maya, Cuba, when a race war erupted. Two of my friends and I were trying to get back to Banes when we were attacked on the train by a militia group and government soldiers. They stopped the train and took us off along with seven other victims into the jungle with the intention of executing us, as I overheard one of them say. Before reaching their destination, a fortunate accident happened that gave us a chance to escape, and we ran for our lives in different directions. One of my friends got separated, and the other two of us headed toward the north shore. My friend with me was shot as the two of us were trying to get away in a small boat. There were three of us when we left La Maya, and I don't know what happened to the other one, whether he escaped or was killed. It's sad because he has a wife and two children, and he was trying to get back to them in Banes. I finally managed to row out of reach of the gunshots and ended up alone in this boat at sea. I was about to lose all hope when your ship found me and rescued me."

"You happened to be in the wrong place at the wrong time, son. You're lucky to be alive. Now, what am I going to do with you? It would be too cruel to throw you back into the ocean, and this ship is certainly not turning back to a Cuban port or any other until it has completed its mission. You're going to have to join my crew until we get to Panama or California, and that may be six months to a year from now. What kind of work can you do? Can you scrub the deck? Can you paint? Can you cook? What can you do to pay for your keep on my ship?"

"I…I am handy with tools, sir, and I know a little about cooking (If you count the teaching his aunts gave him in their kitchen at home in Trench Pen.)."

"Well, we'll see about that. We are short-handed in the galley, so I think we'll use you there for a while. We'll pay you $4.00 a day with half your pay taken out for your room and board. Have any problems with that?" said the captain.

"Why, no sir! …not at all, sir!"

And here, the captain called the first mate over.

"Emsley, take this young man over to see Chef Headley and tell him to put him to work right away in the galley. See what he can do and let him help out if he can."

Chef Headley was short-handed in the galley because one of his assistant cooks got left behind at the last port of call, but when he looked John Graham over and heard him tell of his skimpy cooking experience and zero prior ship training, he was very skeptical about what this new galley help could do.

"Where you from, boy?" he gruffly asked his new hand.

"I'm from Trench Pen, St. Andrews, Jamaica, sir."

"You are Jamaican, eh?" and that seemed to have softened the blow because John Headley was himself a Jamaican cook and was glad to meet a countryman on board the ship.

"What you don't know, then I'll teach you if you got a head for learning, but you are going to have to work hard to earn it."

And with that, he was introduced to the chief cook and began his apprenticeship in the galley; you might call it that. He was given the rest of the evening to rest up and to start his duties the following day. He seemed to have a knack for the work, and he didn't mind the myriad hours of peeling potatoes, cleaning fish, and swabbing the galley floors, for, after two months of diligent work, he was taken into the confidence of Chief Headley and was taught the routines of the galley. He worked very hard, learned the menus, and always paid close attention to his teacher. It was not long before he became an able and reliable assistant chef in the galley.

Now that he had gained the confidence of the head chef, Headley, and his friendship, he tried to find out if there was any news about what was going on back in Cuba. He had kept it to himself, but he was dying to know what had happened to the people he left back there.

"Mr. Headley, I owe my life to your captain and crew for rescuing me from the Atlantic, and I owe a lot to you as well for treating me decently and teaching me everything I know as a beginner chef. But all this time, I have been dying to learn about what happened to my friends in Cuba. It's more than three months, and there must be some way of finding out. Maybe there is an old newspaper article, or maybe there was information over the radio. Can you help me?"

"We all heard the story you told the captain on the first day you were picked up, and I admit I wanted to talk to you about that for some time now, but I didn't; I was waiting until you felt like bringing the subject up. I know if I was in your place I would have been damn anxious to know what happened, so I took the liberty of saving some articles for you from the St. Lucian and Brazilian newspapers when we stopped there to refuel some time ago. I'll show them to you when we retire to
the crew's quarters later. It looks like a lot of bad things happened in Cuba back there in May, June, and July."

"I can't thank you enough for whatever information you are able to get for me. I really would like to know what happened in Cuba during the time after I was rescued."

Later, Chief Headley pulled out some clippings and an article he had saved from a pro-Cuba libre newspaper regarding the "Massacre." It was an English translation of what took place:

"*Starting on May 20, 1912, throughout Cuba, especially in Oriente province, Cienfuegos, and Santa Clara, political meetings and public demonstrations took place among the Afro-Cuban communities in protest. Reactions were swift and cruel, however. Anti-black hatred was stirred up by the white media; enemies of the Partido Independiente de Color (PIC) exploited the opportunity to arouse in whites the fear of blacks rising up and taking over the country; white militias and mobs were formed; Jose Miguel Gomez, head of the government of Cuba dispatched the army into Oriente with the mission to "search and destroy the PIC and their sympathizers who were concentrated in Oriente. Suddenly, it was dangerous to be dark-skinned in Cuba. Men and women were attacked by white militias as they were walking home from work or visiting with friends. On May 23, police near Cienfuegos shot to death 8 peaceful Negroes. Black skin was enough reason to suspect a person and enough reason to execute them. Bodies of suspected rebels were left hanging outside the towns for moral reasons, and severed heads were placed on the sides of the road and railroad tracks so passengers could see them. President Gomez reinstituted concentration camps in the Oriente province, and thousands of black families who were not massacred were forced into them. These conditions led Afro-Cuban veterans from the War of Independence and farmers and peasants, though ill-equipped, to retaliate against such injustices. The result was an increase in the massacres of May and June 1912.*

The worst one took place in La Maya on May 31ˢᵗ when the military inflicted horrendous carnage. General Carlos Mendieta had invited journalists to witness the efficiency of the army's new machine guns, which he fired on hundreds of peaceful Afro-Cuban peasants, killing them all. Entire families have machine-gunned their bodies, and for days, vultures circled over the area, attracted by the corpses. In one night in Guantanamo, Mayor Pedro Perez, a former slave bounty hunter, ordered the massacre of 50 Afro-Cubans. The slaughter spread to the towns throughout Oriente province, including Yateras, Guantanamo, Alto Songo, Micara, Santiago de Cuba, etc., and by the end of June 1912, when the massacre was done, more than 12,000 blacks and mulattos were slaughtered, including many of the PIC leaders, especially Evarista Estenoz and Antonio Yvonnet, who were the main targets and who were shot point blank in the back of their heads by Cuban army officers when they were captured. It was a horrendous example of unjustified government use of force to silence the voice and will of its African-Cuban population."

After reading the article, John wanted to cry, for he never thought that such cruelty was possible in Cuba, or anywhere, to people who had done no wrong, people who, in fact, had fought bravely and given their lives for Cuban independence and only asked to be treated equally and fairly. Then it came to him that his Cuban friends might have been victims, too. What happened, he wondered, to the Ramos family, Francisco, Gloria, Maria, and Julio, and to Pedro, who was separated in the woods when they were escaping from the militia? He may never know the answer. If only there was some way that he could find out.

"Weren't you staying with some friends or relatives in Banes, Cuba, before the massacre occurred?" asked Headley.

"Yes, Carl Brewster and his wife Estelle; I am sure they weren't involved. They didn't even want me to leave the plantation when I left to go with my Cuban friends to spend some time in La Maya."

"Then why don't you write them? I am sure a UFC mail carrier delivers mail there to their people."

"But there's no mail pick up on this ship. How will I mail such a letter?"

"When we come to port in Chile, we can mail it there. In the meantime, you can write letters to them and to any of your relatives who are wondering what happened to you, and when we get to port, you can mail them all at the same time."

They were now at sea for almost four months since he was rescued, and the ship was now passing through the Strait of Magellan, a channel 350 miles long and 1.1 miles wide that cuts through the southern part of Chile, saving them some time rather than going around the more dangerous Cape Horn, which lies south of the southernmost tip of South America and is fraught with the most dangerous winds and tides. Magellan Strait is also dangerous, but with excellent piloting, it's not a problem. John was able to see from the deck the myriads of penguins and some giant whales that are natural to this region. He was also able to see Fort Bulnes way off in the distance, which was built by the Chilean government in 1843 to protect the strait.

After leaving the Strait, they traveled north along the west coast of South America until they reached Valparaiso port, Chile. There, John was able to mail the letters he wrote to his uncle Cyrus Graham, Carl and Estelle Brewster, his sponsor Samuel Brewster, and his aunts Sarah and Beulah to let them know he was alive and only the spirit of his father John Graham, Sr. and the mercy of God saved him from disaster in Cuba and on the Atlantic Ocean, but he was rescued by a ship and hopes to be in Panama soon when he will write again. In his letter to Carl, he regretted not taking his and his wife's advice to stay on the plantation and asked Carl if he could find out for him what happened to his friends Pedro Augustin and Julio Ramos, who worked at the Banes Mill with him during the last Zafra season. Unfortunately, he told Carl Francis Warner, who had left with him to go to La Maya, was killed when they were trying to escape from the militia on their way back to Banes, while he was lucky to get away in a small boat that drifted out to sea where he was rescued. He wanted to know if his friends survived the massacre. In all the letters, he gave his Uncle Cyrus's address in Panama as his return address. He knew that Cyrus would hold the mail for him when the responses came back.

After mailing the letters, they returned to the ship and sailed for Hawaii to deliver their shipment of manufactured goods from New York and receive a large shipment of tons of sugar and pineapples from Hawaii to transport back to New York.

Several days were spent in Honolulu port, and instead of returning to New York via South America and the Strait of Magellan, the captain's instructions were to unload his cargo for New York at the port of Balboa, C.Z. from where the shipment was to be transported by P.R.R. to Colon port and then shipped from there to New York. The Panama Canal was not scheduled to be opened for at least another year (1914), and the overland shipment via the Panama Railroad would save several days, possibly a week or more. Also, at Balboa, the ship would pick up passengers and cargo from Panama to sail to San Francisco, which was a route that was still being used to move cargo and passengers from the Atlantic coast to California.

The detour to Balboa port was convenient for John Graham since he was planning to return to Panama as soon as he was able to. It was now October 17th when the ship left Honolulu port and was nearing Balboa when the captain sent for him.

"Son, we'll be making port soon in Balboa, and I suppose you will be disembarking there and parting company with us?"

"Yes, captain, I'm going back to my Uncle Cyrus in Caledonia, Panama."

"I should think he would be happy to see you after what you've been through."

"Captain, I can't thank you enough for all you have done for me. You don't know how grateful I am to you and your crew for saving my life. I will be in your debt forever."

"It was the right thing to do, lad; moreover, you turned out to be quite a good assistant chef in the galley, I'm told. Anytime you want to sign up with me in the future, I will be glad to take you on my ship. By the way, stop by the bursar before you leave the ship and pick up the rest of your pay coming to you. You earned it, and it will come in handy, I'm sure."

"Thank you very much, sir."

"And remember, in the future, stay out of the Atlantic Ocean -- one miracle is enough for one lifetime."

After he left the captain's quarters, he went by Chef Headley to thank him for everything he had taught him and had done for him and to tell him he hoped to see him again someday. They exchanged addresses and promised to correspond with each other.

Chapter XI: Return to Panama and News of Cuban Friends

On the morning of October 19, 1912, the ship, SS Bayano, docked in Balboa port where, after clearing with Panama port authorities, John headed straight for Caledonia, Panama City. When he reached his uncle's apartment in Muller's building, there was a sign on the door (presumably left there for him): 'Gone to Grant's Barbershop, will be back in a couple of hours.'

He remembered where Walter Grant's barbershop was on Central Avenue near 24th Street, so he headed over there. When he arrived, sure enough, his uncle was sitting in the barber's chair getting his hair cut. As he entered the barbershop and Uncle Cyrus saw him, he was so happy that he got out of the chair and reached out to him with open arms.

"John, John Graham Jr., is that you, son? I can't believe my eyes!"

"Yes, Uncle, it's me, your nephew, John; it's so good to see you, too!"

And they hugged each other and showed some emotion which men ordinarily are reluctant to display. Then Uncle Cyrus turned to Mr. Grant, the owner and head barber.

"Walter, you know my nephew, John. He used to come in here a couple of years ago."

"Yes, I remember him. Did you say he just came back from Cuba, where they had that race riot and all that killing four or five months ago? Was he there when all that was going on?"

"Yes," said Uncle Cyrus, "and he went through hell, but thank God he is safe now."

"My boy," said Walter Grant, "I, too, am glad to see you. You know Panama may have its problems, but it was far safer than it was in Cuba for a black man during the last five months and is still much safer today. Come, let me finish with your uncle, and he can take you home. I am sure you two must have a lot to talk about. Have a seat, son, this won't take long."

When barber Grant finished cutting his hair, Cyrus and John went home to the apartment, and the first thing Cyrus did was share with him a letter that he had received from Cuba almost four months ago. It was a letter he had received from Carl and Estelle Brewster in Banes, Cuba, telling him how worried they were that he had not returned from a place called La Maya, Cuba, where he had gone for a visit and that they believed something terrible had happened to him. Frantic as he was at that time when he had received John's letter mailed to him from Valparaiso, Chile, all fears and anxieties were lifted, and joy and relief took their place instead. When Cyrus told him that, John began to relate to him again the whole story without leaving out any details about his experience and his ordeal in Cuba. Cyrus listened intently, and afterward, he appreciated the impact and the effect that it had on his nephew's countenance and young life.

"You don't know how worried we all were about you, son," he said to him, "your aunts and I kept praying every day for you and that someway, somehow, you were safe. Words can't tell how glad I was to learn that you had managed to survive."

"Uncle, I feel so lucky and happy to be alive that sometimes I think it was more than luck; I believe that while I was drifting alone out there in the ocean, someone was watching over me."

"John Graham Sr..it's John Graham Sr., it was your father looking after his son, making sure you were safe, that's who it was."

And John could only shake his head in agreement, and for a few seconds, his mind wandered back to the moment at sea when he was desperate, and he swore that he had heard his father's voice speaking to him: 'Pray, my son, miracles do happen.'
"Yes," said John after hesitating for a few seconds, "I believe my father was watching over me."

"Now you have to write to your aunts and let them know yourself you are alive and well."

"But, Uncle, I did write them. I also wrote Carl and Estelle in Cuba and Samuel Brewster the same time I wrote you from the ship," said John, "and I mailed all the letters at the same time from Valparaiso, Chile as well. I gave them your address here in Panama as my return address; you should have received responses from them by now."

"Their letters have not arrived as yet, but since I received mine, I am sure theirs will arrive any day now. I know you are anxious to hear from the Brewsters in Cuba, so I'll make sure I check the mail first thing Monday morning."

It was Saturday afternoon, and Uncle Cyrus knew that John was tired and could use some rest. They fixed up something to eat with the provisions they purchased in the little market on the way home, and after eating dinner, Uncle Cyrus stepped out for a little while, leaving John to get some rest.

The following day, Sunday, October 27, 1912, Uncle Cyrus thought it was a good idea if they went to church that morning and gave thanks for their blessings and for their good fortune. They got up early and went to the 11 a.m. service at Elder James W. Burke's church on 24th Street East, which was not too far from Muller's Building, a few blocks east of Central Avenue.

After the service, Cyrus decided to take John with him for a walk on Central Avenue up to Santa Ana Plaza. There's a popular park there where West Indians usually gather and share information. Churches, lodge halls, barbershops, markets, bars, and parks are some of the places where West Indians meet up to socialize with friends and get their news and information about what's going on locally and back home. As Uncle Cyrus and John reached the park and they sat down on a park bench with a good view of the traffic and passersby along Central Avenue, Marcus Dinkley, a friend of Cyrus', came and sat down beside them. He is an old friend who lives in Chorrillo, and on Sunday afternoons, he likes to come to the park-like Uncle Cyrus and meet old friends. They had a lot to talk about.

"Hello, Cyrus, ah knew ah would run into you, and how things no?"

"Things are alright, although they could be a little bit better."

"You know who I ran into the other day?"

"Who so?"

"Rufus Donovan, remember we were already here when he came in '04?"

"Yes, and didn't he go back home at one time?"

"But he came back. He said things were too hard back home in Kingston; there's no work, and people are struggling to survive, so he came back about a year ago. He's been working for the Dredging Division down in the Gamboa area since. I tell you, Cyrus, I don't know what is going to become of us when this Canal job finishes."

"Don't worry, we'll survive. If you have good skills, I don't care where you are, you'll find a job. Besides, what a lot of us need to do while we are working is to put away a little for tam bran season. Even a little from a little is still something. Some of us have been here for nearly 10 years and don't have anything to show for it."

"That's good and well for you to say, Cyrus. You have always been one to save a penny, but everybody isn't like you."

"Maybe, but remember, one day, don't cry to me if you find yourself in a fix and you don't have a penny to your name."

"All right, Ben Franklin, I have been forewarned."

Just then, another West Indian, Fitzroy James, joined them.

"Make room for a good man to join you." And he tried to squeeze in between them.

"I don't see any good man," said Cyrus, "Rufus, you see any good man around here besides you and me?"

"Come on, Cyrus, don't be a mean so-and-so," protested Fitzroy.

"Oh, you even know my name, son of a gun, ain't that something!"

"Alright, I know where you are coming from, 'Good evening, Rufus and Cyrus. Could I please join you on this beautiful afternoon here on this park bench?"

"That's a lot better; make yourself comfortable," replied Cyrus.

After they all had a good little laugh out of the exchange, Fitzroy, who had just come from the direction of Casco Viejo, shared an observation with them.

"I see them doing some type of road construction back there in the Palacio and las Bovedas area. I wonder what they are up to?"

"In Chorrillo, too, I noticed them doing some road construction," added Marcus. "Are they repaving the roads or something?"

"They are laying down rail tracks," said Uncle Cyrus. They are building a rail system for tram cars to run along Central Avenue all the way to the Palacio and north all the way past Bella Vista into Sabanas."

"And what about Chorrillo?" asked Marcus.

"You see that corner over there where "C" Street meets Central Avenue. They are going to lay street rails turning from Central Avenue onto "C" Street, which will turn into "B" Street, and go all the way west through Chorrillo into the Canal Zone. That branch is going to go through Balboa up to that new town sight they are building for West Indians and their families."

"Cyrus, how do you know so much about this," asked Fitzroy.

"I must know since I've seen the plans. By next year, 1913, you're going to see tram cars running all along here going north and south up and down Central Avenue."

"That will be a boon for poor people," said Fitzroy, "they going to be able to go sightseeing all the time and visit places instead of staying home."

"Not only that, but business is also going to prosper, and this place is going to have a lot more traffic in Panama City."

"That's progress," said Cyrus, "and who knows where it is going to lead. People will get to where they want to go much easier and cheaper: to church, to school, to work, to shop, to visit, you name it. This place is going to grow because of it."

"As you say, Cyrus, that's progress, alright; hooray for the tramcars."

By now, it was late afternoon, and Cyrus got up to bid his friends goodbye.

"It was nice seeing you, Marcus, and Fitzroy; maybe we can meet up again next Sunday."

"So long, Cyrus," both friends replied in unison, "see you next week."

Cyrus and John headed back north on Central Avenue toward the Muller building.

That evening in the apartment, as they prepared to call it a night, Cyrus noticed that John was moody and somewhat sad.

"What's matter, son, what's bothering you?"

"I can't stop thinking about my friends in Cuba. I would give anything to know what happened to them and if I will ever see them again."

"Go to sleep, son; we'll know tomorrow or very soon."

The next day after work, Uncle Cyrus made a special trip to the post office, and sure enough, the letters had arrived. He came home and shared the news with John, who couldn't wait to read the letters. However, the Brewster's response was not very encouraging:

"Dear John,

> While we were happy to hear that you had managed to escape from your pursuers and were rescued by a friendly sea captain, your friends were not so lucky. The bloodthirsty killers attacked the people

of La Maya and Songa and most of Oriente province with rifles and machine guns, and they massacred thousands of innocent farmers and their families. We are sorry to tell you that the friends you were staying with when you visited La Maya were all killed in the massacre. They didn't stand a chance. The only good news I can give you is that your friend Pedro managed to elude the militia and made it back to Banes and is reunited with his wife and two children.

We don't know if you plan to return to Cuba, but let us know if you do. At any rate, we shipped your personal things to Samuel Brewster in Colon for you because we thought you might need them.

Keep well, John, with our blessings.

Carl and Estelle"

When he read those lines, there were tears in his eyes. He was fond of the Ramos family, especially Maria, Julio's sister, for whom he had developed a warm affection. Uncle Cyrus tried to console him, but the hurt had to run its course.

"I'll never go back to Cuba again," he said, "there is nothing there for me now."

After he read all his letters and thanked them all for their kind thoughts and his aunts, especially for their love, he and Uncle Cyrus sat down and had a serious talk about his future. Cyrus assured him that he could take as much time as he needed to make up his mind about what he wanted to do, that as his nephew, he would always be taken care of by him as if he were his own son, and if he needed his advice he only had to ask.

Chapter XII: Settling Down in Colon

He thought about looking for work as a cook now that he had some experience with Chef Headley on board the S.S. Bayano; he also thought about looking for work as a carpenter since he had experience in Banes under Carl Brewster, and he thought about something Samuel Brewster had said when he responded to his letter written from the ship, that he could always use a good young man like him in one of his business ventures if John was interested and decided not to go back to Cuba. He was never clear what he meant in the letter, but he had to see him anyway to retrieve the things that his brother Carl had sent from Cuba in his care, so when he went to Colon for his things, he could find out what he had in mind. A few days after receiving the letters, he told Uncle Cyrus he was going to Colon to see Mr. Samuel Brewster and retrieve his things, and maybe he might have another job offer for him.

The following Monday morning, he was on the 7:30 a.m. train to Colon on his way to retrieve his personal belongings sent from Cuba by Carl and Estelle Brewster. When he reached the office on Front Street, the sign on the window was slightly changed. It said:

United Fruit Company Agent

&

Real Estate Broker

SAMUEL R. BREWSTER

Samuel Brewster himself was at the office door to greet him.

"Welcome back, son. I am happy to see you again. Come in … come in."

And John was ushered into the inner office, where Brewster offered him a seat, and they warmly conversed.

"I understand that you will not be returning to Cuba. I am sorry about that, and I can understand your feelings after what you went through."

"Thank you for your understanding," replied John, "and I want you to know I appreciate everything both you and your brother have done for me."

"Don't even think about that; we are like family, as Carl told you. When your father, your uncle Carl, Estelle, and I were children growing up in Kingston, your grandfather was an idol to us in the community, and we were like brothers and sisters."

"Yes, Carl and Estelle told me."

"Good. I have the package that they sent to you in my care. Don't forget to take it with you when you are leaving."

"Thanks again for taking care of it."

"That's nothing, but let me ask you, what do you intend to do now that you are remaining in Panama? I know you are not intending to go back to working on the Canal."

"Never," said John, "but I'm a good carpenter and a cook, and I am handy with my hands."

"Remember when we first met on the boat coming from Kingston, and I told you never to keep your eggs all in one basket and that I wore several hats and was planning to go into real estate? Well, I have acquired some properties right here in Colon since you left to go to Cuba. I own a few houses on 10th and 7th streets, and I may still acquire more property. The only problem is that they are a handful for me to maintain."

"What do you mean a handful to maintain?"
"Well, I may be spreading myself a little too thin. I need good people I can trust to work for me and look after my properties."

"Are you offering me a job, Mr. Brewster?"

"Why not? I need a superintendent to take care of my buildings for me. Would you like to tackle the job?"

"Sir, you know how badly I need a job, but you have to tell me what is involved before I can give you an answer."

"First of all, I will need you to be on the location 24 hours a day to take care of emergencies such as repairs as needed, to see to the removal of waste, to make sure the water and electrical systems are maintained and working properly and, lastly, to keep me always informed about how things are going. To do all this, of course, you'll live rent-free in an apartment in one of the buildings, and you'll set up a 24-hour call service for the tenants."

"How much will you pay me to do the job? And what about time off and vacation? When do I get to rest?"

"I'll pay you $5/day in addition to free rent, and you can take 2 weeks vacation per year, but only one week at a time. Do you want the job?"

"Yes, I'll take it; when do you want me to start?"

"You can take today and tomorrow to decide and report on Wednesday to start. Sundays will be your day off."

"Okay," replied John as they shook hands, pending the written contract.

"I'll try to help you as much as I can," said Brewster. "Whatever you need to know about the real estate business, I will teach you, and you will also try to learn as much as you can about such things as building supplies, procurement, contractors, government regulations, etc. I think you will do fine," said Brewster.

After they took care of the paperwork and the job agreement, Mr. Brewster took John over to see the properties on 10th street, three 2-story frame buildings with a confectionary shop on the ground floor of one building and the next two buildings next to it on the same block, in the second building on the ground floor was located John's new apartment as the super.

The fourth building on 7th street was a frame building, as were 99% of all the buildings in Colon at that time. The clients were a mix of West Indian Canal Zone workers and Latinos.

John returned to Panama City and gave his uncle the news about his new position and plans to move to Colon on

Wednesday. Uncle Cyrus never objected to anything John wanted to do, although he would always give him useful advice.

"Son, you know taking care of 1 building is a big responsibility, much more than 4 buildings. You going to have your hands filled."

"I know, Uncle, but I'm willing to try anything to get ahead. Besides, the pay is $5/day, and my rent is free. I can save a lot of money in a couple of years, and I am still going to come and visit you as often as I can."

"I know you will, son. You are growing into a man and learning to take care of yourself just as your father wanted. Soon, I won't be around, so it's just as well you learn to take care of yourself."

"What do you mean, Uncle?"

"Next year, the canal will be finished, and when it's completed, I am planning to go back to Jamaica to live. I've been planning that ever since I came here. I'm beginning to miss Jamaica, you know."

"What are you going to do when you go back home?"

"Don't you worry; the government, as well as private companies, can always use a construction worker like me to build things. I know masonry and carpentry too well. I'll get by; besides, I saved up a little. Anyway, that's a year or so from now, and I'll be here in the meantime whenever you need me."

On Wednesday morning, he left bright and early to go to Colon and assume his new job. Letters were sent to all the tenants by the management to let them know who the new super was, his address, and how to reach him in cases of emergency.

The first month went smoothly. There he was in the heart of Colon, a super for a Johnny-come-lately landlord. He was first a pinche on the Canal, then a carpenter in Cuba, then a cook on a ship, and now a super in Colon. What next, John Graham?

The next year, 1913, was a challenging one. He never knew there could be so many complaints and the service buzzer and telephone could ring so much, and that there were so many things that could go wrong in one building, let alone 4, but he hung in there, repairing leaks and cracks and clogs, fixing faucets and fixtures and, worst of all, dealing with unpleasant and sometimes raucous tenants. After six months, he thought he deserved a raise, and when he told Mr. Brewster that, he promptly increased his pay to $7/day. Now, he just had to stick it out, for his bank account was also growing nicely as his endurance was.

He found ways to cope, and he found, too, that not all the tenants were bad. He got to know Mrs. Ruby in apartment 3, who treated him so well that he would visit her apartment often and sometimes would stay for breakfast afterward.

"How come a nice young man like you is still single?" she would ask him, "Don't you want to get married?"

"I am single, and I plan to stay that way for a long time," was his answer.

And she didn't mind, for that meant that she didn't have to contend with jealous wives or girlfriends.

"That's all right with me, honey," she said to him, "I ain't looking for no husband neither to tie me down."

She knew what she was saying because she was a widow who had been married twice, and her last husband died and left her a comfortable income on which she depended, along with a share in a confectionary store where she worked in the building next door. She is planning to go back home to Trinidad soon, but in the meantime, John Graham helps to satisfy her lonely needs. So, they had a mutual understanding.

Now, this should be enough to occupy any hardworking young man's spare time, but he found out that there was another lonely housewife, Mrs. Cecilia Archer, in a building on 6th Street who also needed his attention from time to time.

"When are you coming by again to see me, John Graham?" she said to him as he was leaving her apartment late one night.

"You know I got to be careful because your shippy husband might come home at any time. I 'tekking' a big chance with you, you know."

"Don't worry about that; I know my husband's schedule better than you. Come Wednesday, I am 'going' fix something special for you."

He couldn't resist the temptation, and the next Wednesday night, he came knocking at her door. She was, of course, expecting him and wore her sexiest negligee and sweet scents and body cream. At the appointed time, 10 p.m., she heard that special knock, one hard, 3 soft, 2 hard, then a pause, then repeats, one hard, 3 soft, 2 hard. She knew it was him and she opened the door. He came into the dimly lit apartment and was immediately overcome and sensitized by the aroma and her taunting appearance. He followed her slithering form as she led him into the bedroom. There was no point in wasting time since the iron was so hot, and they both quickly undressed and succumbed to their animal natures. If there was any thought about an absent spouse before that, it was now cast into utter oblivion; anyway, her husband must have gone away for a very long time for her to be so ravenous. For hours, they rode their passion's crests and troughs without seeming to tire, but as they ravished the forbidden fruit into the dawn, suddenly, their stolen bliss was interrupted. There was a sound of someone at the door of the apartment. As if a sudden shock of adrenalin went swiftly through her brain, the last sweet ebbs of erotica were aborted when she suddenly jumped up from the bed in horrid fright.

"My husband…my husband...my husband is at the door!" she said to John, "You got to go…you got to go!"

John, grasping the meaning, could only say to himself, "No nooky in this whole world is worth dying for," and he grabbed his clothes and shoes (he'll dress later) and jumped through the back window; luckily, one flight, to the ground and ran all the way from 6th to 10th street before he stopped and pulled himself together.

Back at the apartment on 6th Street, while John was making his escape, Cecilia's husband, even though he opened the door lock with his key, still couldn't get in. Fortunately for the two lovers, she had put a metal bar reinforcement in place so the door could not move easily from outside. As her husband, who is very strong, was about to break down the door, she called out to him.

"Charlie, Charlie, a coming…don't break it down…a beg you please."

And she removed the bar on the inside so he could get in, and he bolted in with a rage.

"Where is the S.O.B.? I know you got a man in here; where is the S.O.B.?"

"No, honey, there's no man in here. It is only me. I bar the door for my protection so thieves can't break in."

But he knew she was lying.

"And why are you wearing a black negligee, and you smell of perfume? Woman, you must be tek me for a fool!"

And he rushed into the bedroom and saw the bed all tussled up and smelling funky like you know what. Then he turned to her, full of rage, and she screamed out, begging for her life.

"Charlie, don't kill me; I love you, darling…don't kill me, please. You always leave me here alone by myself for months and months. I've been cooped up here all the time, missing you and needing you. I can't help it. You mustn't leave me alone."

Somehow, his rage was assuaged, for the next day, there was no domestic killing reported; there was only one repentant housewife with some bruises after she had dodged a bullet the night before.

A week after that incident, her husband had her pack her things, and he took her away from there. The story goes that he took her back to Belize with him to live with his family, and she was never unfaithful again.

John Graham, on the other hand, had learned a valuable lesson: "Don't mess around with married women if you want to live a long life."Anyway, he still had his reliable and less dangerous Ruby in apartment 3 on 10th Street where he lived, and she was as accommodating as always when, a few days later, he paid her a visit.

After a very pleasant night of lovemaking the following morning at breakfast, she broke the news to him.

"Baby, I'm selling my interest in the store and moving back to Trinidad."

"Is something wrong, Ruby, that you not telling me about?"

"No, nothing wrong; I'm just tired, and I think it's time for me to go back home. I got a piece of property back home in Trinidad, you know, and I want you to come and live with me."

"Come to Trinidad and live with you? Ruby, remember what I told you when we first met? I am not looking to get married, and you even said to me you didn't want to be tied down either."

"Don't pay me any mind; I was just joking. I wanted to see how you would react. You not angry, are you?"

"No, Ruby, I am not angry. I still care for you a lot, but I am not ready to make a move like that. That doesn't mean to say I can't come to Trinidad and visit you if that's alright with you."

"You mean that, John?"

"Yes, I do. Leave me your address before you go. But you still didn't say when you leaving."

"I'm leaving next month, June 10, 1913."

"We still have about three weeks before you go. It's not like you're leaving tomorrow, and remember, I'm right here if you need me for anything in the meantime."

So, in the next few weeks, they didn't waste too much time. John must have visited Ruby two or three times a week up to the last day, and he helped her with her packing and arrangements through Brewster travel agency to book her trip home. So when Ruby left, of course, he missed her for a while;

then he settled down to serious work and taking care of Brewster's properties.

After Ruby left, the rest of the year was quiet for John Graham as he tried to keep out of mischief, just working and saving his pennies and being as thrifty as possible to improve his modest bank account. He didn't hang out in bars and brothels as some citizens did. First, that would squander his money, and second, it was dangerous. Just the other day, he was reading about a riot between U. S. soldiers and Panamanian policemen.

There were numerous fights in bars and brothels, especially whenever U.S. servicemen came into town off the bases – they don't respect local police and local customs and often provoke racial conflicts in such venues. One of his own tenants was injured in one of those melees, so John Graham stays clear of such places.

Chapter XIII: Uncle Cyrus' Last Days in Panama

Blowing up of the Gamboa dam (Google)

A few Sundays each month, John visited his uncle in Panama, who was always glad to see him. He was supposed to visit Uncle Cyrus on Sunday, October 12, 1913, but because it was a holiday weekend, he had gone to Panama a day earlier on the evening train. That Saturday, October 11, 1913, was the day that President Wilson blew up the Gamboa dike, which was the last obstruction remaining to join the waters of the Atlantic and the Pacific oceans. That explosion meant that it wouldn't be long before the Canal would be completed and officially opened by the U. S. for commercial traffic. Saturday evening, when he arrived in Panama later that night, some workers were gathered in the Tropical bar on Central Avenue celebrating, and Uncle Cyrus took him there to join in the celebration now that he was old enough. There were several of Cyrus's friends and co-workers waiting there, ready to greet them.

"Hi Cy, busy day, huh?" said one greeter who sat near the entrance.

"Come on in and join the party, Cy," said the bartender as they walked in.

And greetings went around the room, and glasses and mugs and bottles were tipped as the gathering was making merry. As they took their seats, the discussion that was already in progress continued.

"So they blasted the dikes at 2 o'clock today," said one digger.

"Yes, man," said another worker, "all the way from Washington, President Wilson pressed a button, and the dam went up, filling the canal with all that water from the Atlantic Ocean that was being held back by the Gamboa dikes."

"Crowds lined the banks of Culebra Cut to see the spectacle," said another, "I was one of them."

"Tell us about it," said another.

"It was a gigantic roar as they discharged over 1,600 pounds of dynamite, sending a shower of water, mud, and rocks high into the sky in a heavy cloud of smoke. In no time, Culebra Cut was filled to the level of Gatun Lake; man, it was some spectacle!"

"At last, the damn canal a finish, thank God!" said one man in the corner.

"First, they goin' send in the dredges to clear up the debris and make sure it's deep enough," remarked another worker, "but for all practical purposes, the heavy digging is about over."

"And now that the end of construction is in sight, I hope you all realize that day after tomorrow, thousands of us if we didn't get notice already, are going to be laid off because they won't be needing us anymore. I don't hear anybody talking about that."

"Well, we knew it had to end someday for most of us anyway. We sign a contract, you know."

"Well, I don't mind that so much," added another, "but when I think about the poor souls who lost their lives digging it, I feel sorry for their families."

Then Cyrus got up and spoke.

"On that last point, the white man may not give a damn how many of us died building his damn canal, but we West Indians have a right to care, and I demand that we all raise our glasses and make a toast honoring all of our brothers and sisters who gave their lives digging the Panama Canal."

"And let me add to that, brother Cyrus," said another sitting next to him, "we going to drink also in honor of all those who were crippled as well or who lost a leg or an arm for that damn ditch."

"And more than that," said another, "let us remember the wives who stayed at home waiting for husbands who went to work in the morning and never came home again."

"And add to that," said another, "all the children who had a father one night and the next day were fatherless because of that canal."

"Now let us all raise our glasses," said Uncle Cyrus, "Here's to all our fallen, maimed, and crippled brothers and sisters who paid the highest price in the building of the Panama Canal. May we never forget them, and may the world never forget the sacrifices that they made."

There wasn't an empty glass in that Tropical bar, and they all drank and shook hands and celebrated in their own way the achievement of the 8th Wonder of the Modern World, the Panama Canal.

The next day, Uncle Cyrus made it clear and reminded his nephew that after the official celebration of the opening of the Panama Canal was over, he was returning to Jamaica, and that would be sometime in the following year.

The year 1914 began like any other year; only it was shaped by five significant events that took place. The first event occurred on April 1, 1914, when the Panama Canal Zone structure was changed from one that was run by a military Isthmian Canal Commission to one run by a civilian Canal Zone *Government under a governor appointed by the President of the U.S.. As the major construction work on the

Canal was now completed and the Canal was being transitioned over, thousands of construction workers were laid off, and most either returned to their country or sought refuge in Colon and Panama City. Approximately half of the workforce was kept on by the newly structured Canal Zone government to work in the various divisions that would maintain the Panama Canal operation under the governor and his administration.

Whether it was a blessing or not, West Indians in Colon seemed to manage in spite of the massive layoffs. In the private sector, many ships that were entering Limon Bay on the Atlantic side would stop for coaling and supplies before proceeding, which benefitted Colon commercially; tourist trade was growing and gave rise to the construction by the PRR Co. of a large hotel (Washington Hotel) built of concrete and cement blocks and consisting of 1,000 rooms and modern conveniences; the Cristobal dock works, the cold storage plant, the power plant, water plant, printing press, laundry, commissary, fire and sanitation departments, transportation division, small business, stores, nightclubs, restaurants, sports and entertainment venues provided ample employment opportunities that helped Colon to remain somewhat stable and even to grow for a while.

The second big event that occurred in 1914 was World War I when Austria-Hungary attacked Serbia on July 29, 1914, in retaliation for the assassination of Archduke Ferdinand and Duchess Sophie of Austria, embroiling almost every nation into a global conflict, "the War to End All Wars," that broke out on August 1, 1914, when Germany, an ally of Austria-Hungary, launched a ground attack on Russia's ally, France through Belgium. Many of America's friends were involved in the conflict, and although the U.S. claimed exceptionalism and tried to remain neutral, there was always the specter that World War I could draw her into it somehow, so there was that fear even in 1914-1915 especially as German U-boats were roaming the Atlantic Ocean.

The third event of 1914 was the opening of the Panama Canal which was scheduled to be officially opened on August

15, 1914 -- and there were projected plans for an elaborate gala celebration with speeches and fanfare and numerous invited officials, dignitaries, foreign guests, and celebrities -- but, unfortunately, none of that took place. Everything was canceled due to the sudden outbreak of World War I, as previously mentioned. The elaborate canal celebration was out of the question. However, there was still a modest passage of note of the S.S. Ancon on August 15, 1914, signaling the official opening of the Panama Canal.

The fourth significant event that took place that year happened in September 1914. It was the departure of Uncle Cyrus from Panama for Jamaica. He had written to Sarah and Beulah to tell them he was arriving in Kingston on the 14th, and on Saturday, September 11, 1914, John Graham was at the pier in Cristobal to see his dear uncle sail for home, Jamaica. For Uncle Cyrus, it was the end of an era that began back in 1888 when he and later his beloved brother, John's father, had embarked on their canal adventure. He was tired, and, in a way, he was glad it was over for him; he was going back to his country to live out the rest of his years with some good and perhaps some not-so-good memories. He embraced his nephew as they said goodbye.

"John, you're a man now; you're on your own; you must take good care of yourself. And remember, you always have a home in Jamaica with me and your aunts, if ever and whenever you get tired of this country and you decide you want to come back home. I leave you to make that decision for yourself. Give Samuel Brewster my regards and tell him I thank him for everything he has done for you, and please don't forget to write us."

And as he watched the ship sail out of the harbor, he knew he was going to miss his uncle.

Chapter XIV: The Last Adventure

The fifth, and perhaps the most significant, event that took place in the life of John Graham Jr. was his meeting with Marianne Dupre. To get to that, though, first, he must meet Evaline or, more correctly, Mrs. Evaline Thomas, Marianne's sister.

One day in late October, he was busy doing some repairs to the interior of the building he happened to live in when he was noticed by Evaline, one of his neighbors who seemed to have her eyes on him.

"You are the hardest working man I ever saw." She said to him. "Don't you know that all work and no play is bad for your health?"

"Is that your medical advice, Dr. ….?"

"It's Mrs. Evaline Thomas and all I'm saying is it's a lovely day outside, and there's a big parade passing by. Why don't you come outside and see your brothers march? It will take your mind off of work for a little while."

He suddenly remembered that a few years ago, he had become an apprentice Freemason with the help of his uncle and that he was proud of his status then, though he never continued active membership. He went outside with Evaline to look at the parade, and it rekindled his affinity for the brotherhood. They looked so fine in their regalia. There, at the head of the parade, was the grand marshal with all his decorations, then there was another marshal carrying a banner, followed by a master mason, a senior warden, then guards and sword bearers, and banner bearers, followed by the rank and file, and they were doing steps in unison and different formations. It was impressive as they marched up 10th Street toward the Masonic temple at the corner of Bolivar and 10th Street.

"Are you enjoying the parade?" asked Evaline.

"Yes, they're good! And I see that you seem to be enjoying it yourself," he replied.

"I love a parade," she said, "I just like to see the way they step; it is so pretty! We should have more parades in this town to liven things up."

"Yes," said John, "they sure know how to bring out the crowds who are enjoying it."

And as the last rank and file Mason passed by and they turned the corner at Bolivar, John said to her:

"Well, I must get back to work before you start saying I am a lazy carpenter."

"Before you go," said Evaline, "I want to ask you if you would like to come to our church on Sunday. Some good Christian fellowship on Sundays would do you good; besides, there are some fine Christian ladies who would be happy to welcome a single, eligible bachelor like you. And I know you aren't married because you live in a first-floor apartment all by yourself. So can I count on you to come?"

"It's nice of you to invite me," he said, "but I'm not the church-going type, not that I have anything against going to church."

"I hear that same story too many times," she said, "at any rate, here's a flyer about a celebration we are having two weeks from today, that's on a Saturday at the church. There will be entertainment and refreshments, and it's for anybody in the community who wants to attend. Keep the flyer and think about it; it is two weeks from today."

As he returned to work, Mrs. Thomas returned to her apartment to do her housework or whatever she was doing before.

The following Saturday around noon, the super's bell rang, and when he opened the door, there was the most attractive, nicely dressed young lady in her early twenties standing right before him.

"Good afternoon, sir," she said in the sweetest voice you could imagine, "are you the caretaker of this building?"

"Yes, I am the super if that's what you mean."

"Would you be so kind as to help me?"

"Of course I will."

"I have been ringing Mrs. Thomas' apartment, but she doesn't seem to answer. Can you check and see for me if everything is alright?"

"Are you a relative of hers, may I ask?"

"Yes, I am her little sister Marianne Dupre. She was expecting me to come by today," replied the young lady.

He doesn't frequently get such charming young ladies ringing his doorbell, with such a pretty-sounding name and features so fine, so he was eager to comply with her request. He went to Mrs. Thomas' apartment and knocked on the door several times. He called Mrs. Thomas, but to no avail, then he returned to the stranger at the front door.

"I am afraid she is not at home. She could have gone to the market; would you like to wait in my apartment until she returns?"

"O no, thank you, sir," said Marianne, "but could you give her this message about the concert on Saturday for me, please?" And she handed him a note to give to her sister. She then smiled and thanked him for his help before she blithely walked away.

There must have been a canary somewhere in his brain that started tweeting, for he swore he had never seen anyone so beautiful, and she took his breath away. Just then, he thought about the flyer. He closed his door and started to look for the flyer that Mrs. Thomas had given him. He finally found it and read it for the first time:

FIRST BAPTIST CHURCH MUSICAL CELEBRATION
Saturday afternoon, October 24, 1914
2:00 p.m. – 4:00 p.m.
Featuring First Baptist Church Choir
And
Other Distinguished Guest Artists
Refreshments to follow in the church hall
Everyone is invited.

After reading the flyer, he realized the date was next Saturday. Now, although he was not a church-going man, he was sure this time he could make an exception; besides, it was a musical concert and not a regular Sunday service. His real interest was to see Marianne again.

On Saturday afternoon, he got to the church a little late, just as the choir was about to begin the second half of the program, and he was lucky to get a seat in the auditorium, which was almost filled. He looked around to see if he saw her, and lo and behold, there she was, standing in the front row of the choir as the voices opened the second half of the program with the very joyful song, "O Happy Day," that stimulated the audience so much they could barely restrain themselves from joining in. The whole choir was nicely dressed, standing two rows deep facing the audience, and Evaline, too, was in the choir standing behind Marianne and there also were a lot of fine-looking sisters. They followed "O Happy Day" with the songs "Ninety-nine and Nine" and "Jerusalem the Golden." All the hymns and songs were wonderfully delivered by the choir and were enthusiastically received by the audience, but it was not until they got to the song "Love Lifted Me Up" that John Graham was really captivated, for the solo voice was none other than Marianne's. She sounded like an angel, and she was so beautiful! John Graham lost it then. He fell in love! And when the song was over, he was the most enthusiastic applause in the auditorium that day. His enthusiasm didn't go unnoticed either by Marianne. The choir continued with a few more songs and ended with a rousing rendition of "To God be the Glory" that had the audience standing and more than satisfied that they had gotten their money's worth and were very proud that they had such a fine gospel choir.

After the concert, most of the congregation retired downstairs to enjoy a nice buffet that was prepared for them, and the church members, guests, and choir members all came downstairs and mingled. When Evaline saw him, she and

Marianne came over to where he was sitting to thank him for coming.

"We are glad that you could make it to the concert," said Evaline, "how did you enjoy it?"

"Very much, I'm glad I came."

"I want to introduce you to my little sister, Marianne."

"Yes, I know her," replied John, "we already met."

"When? How?" and Marianne interjected herself into the conversation.

"Remember a week ago when I was supposed to come by your apartment?" Marianne said to Evaline, "I found out he was super when he asked me who I came to see, and we spoke to each other. He offered to help me by checking to see if you were at home, and when he found out you weren't home, I gave him a note for you. Don't you remember the note?"

"O yes, that morning I went to the market when you came by. John Graham, you son of a gun, so that is why you came to the concert?"

"Well…, if I told you that wasn't the reason, you wouldn't believe me anyway, so I am not going to say yes or no. Maybe I was going to come anyway."

"Well, you came," said Marianne, "and that's all that matters."

"Marianne, you two sit here and talk while I go and fix plates for the three of us, I'll be right back,"

Evaline went over to the buffet table and had the helpers fix plates and drinks and bring them over to where they were sitting. While she was gone, the two engaged each other in a warm and friendly conversation.

"I didn't know you could sing so well; you have a very beautiful voice," he said to Marianne.

"Thank you very much, John; I am glad you like my singing."

"That is not all I like about you…"

"What else do you like about me?" asked Marianne.

"The way you carry yourself and that pretty smile of yours, I'm sure you must have someone special in your life, like a husband or a fiancée."

"No, I'm not married, how about you? Do you have someone in your life, like a woman or two, that you are dating?" she asked him, "most men are never satisfied, you know."

"Now, why would you think that of me? Can't you just believe that it is possible that I'm different and that I am just an honest and sincere person?"

"Yeah, and stones can talk, and chickens have teeth. Look, maybe you are honest and all that, but it's hard to trust any man these days; they lie and cheat so much."

"Sounds like you are talking from experience, Marianne; did you have a boyfriend who treated you that way?"

"Maybe," she replied.

"Yes, I can tell you had a boyfriend; what happened?"

"Yes, I did, but he is out of my life now. He used to say nice things just like you, and he was very sweet until he got what he wanted. As it turned out, he was just another rascal, and he had two or three other women he was doing the same thing to. I swore I would never trust another man like that again."

"I'm not going to be like him, I promise you, Marianne. I believe two people should get to know each other very well before they commit themselves to a relationship. You must build trust in each other first and know each other well before anything else."

At that moment, Evaline and an attendant came over to the table with several plates of food, and the three of them sat together, chatting and commiserating. When it was about 6:00 p.m., the buffet was over, and they and all the other guests left having had a very enjoyable time. He didn't get a strong commitment from Marianne, but she did agree to see him again.

They dated the following week on a trial basis, you might say. That Saturday night, he took her out to dinner and showed her such a good time that they agreed to continue seeing each other as long as she felt that she could trust him. The next Saturday night following that first date, he went by her house and took her out to a show at a nightclub on Bolivar Street and wined and dined her, then returned with her to her apartment on 9th Street and Melendez. They continued seeing each other, and after a while, she began to trust him more and more, and he started going regularly by her apartment to visit, even if they didn't always go out. In fact, they got so close that sometimes he would stay over till the next morning. She even got him to go to church at least once or twice each month. They were getting to know each other very well now. As a matter of fact, they started to become very intimate.

"You think it's going to work out between us?" she asked him the night when they first made love, and he was so hooked by then because the sex was out of this world that he had but one reply.

"Oh yes, yes, yes…," in heat he gasped, "the grapes… and…the cherry…are so divine… Johnny Baby… is here…to stay…. unless… unless… you… don't… want… me… to…?"

"Oh Lord, yes… yes…" she cut him off in the heat of her passion, "baby wants you to stay… stay… stay…, baby wants you…to stay…so…bad," and that is how their love affair took off in the beginning of the New Year 1915. Sometimes, she would come by his apartment after work on Fridays and stay over and even tidy up his place and cook for him; sometimes, he would go by her place on a Saturday and stay overnight. Their relationship was getting very strong and promised to become a lasting one. They were seen together often when they were not working or he was not away, and even Evaline saw that they were a perfect match for each other.

"When are you two going to do the right thing and tie the knot?" she would tease them whenever the three of them were together.

"We are in no hurry," Marianne would tell her, "In any case, you'll be the first one to know."

And John would concur because he loved Marianne very much. In fact, they had talked about that subject several times when they were alone together and were making plans but had not yet decided on the date and all the details. The year 1915 started out blissfully for John Graham and was going as well as could be expected. He had steady employment, his bank account was gradually growing, and he had found the love of his life.

In the meantime, in the world at large, despite the war in Europe, January 1915 saw the U.S. government sponsor an exposition, The Panama-California Exposition in California, to show off the opening of the Panama Canal. The Americans wanted to celebrate their finest achievement, the 8th wonder of the world, the building of the Panama Canal, and they built grand pavilions, canal replicas, impressive architecture, and sights. There were write-ups in the local newspapers like the Star & Herald, the Workman, and the Colon Independent News. After all, the Canal was the U.S.'s prize jewel, and so was the Isthmus of Panama to most American citizens at the time. The Panama Railroad owned most of Panama and Colon, and the U.S. owned the Panama Railroad. This was the reality of 1915. Although Panama exercised marginal sovereignty, the U.S. was always in control. The Expo was a very successful fair, as far as Americans were concerned, and many American Zonians made the trip to California to see it and brag about it, but you hardly heard any Caribbean immigrants talk about it; they were more concerned with survival and providing food and shelter for their families.

One afternoon in March of 1915, when John had finished some banking in Colon, he stopped in a local restaurant to have a lunch snack before returning home. There, he met a learned gentleman from Barbados, Mr. H. N. Waldron, who championed West Indian causes and published a weekly newspaper called "The Workman." While John was having a sandwich, Mr. Waldron was sitting at a table next to his, and he noticed a copy of a newspaper Mr. Waldron was carrying and had laid aside to partake of the dish that the waiter had just brought him. The headline said, "S.S. Bayano sunk by a German submarine off the coast of Ireland early in the morning of 3/15/1915, with the loss of 370 lives and very few survivors.

"Pardon me, sir," he said to the gentleman, "may I please look at your paper if you do not mind?"

"Why not at all," said Mr. Waldron as he noticed John's intense curiosity in the headlines of the newspaper.

He handed him the paper, and John began to read the article with great intensity, which caught Mr. Waldron's eye.

"Pardon me," said Mr. Waldron, "but I couldn't help noticing how engrossed you seemed to be in that article. Did you know someone on that ship?"

"I served on that ship just two years ago. I worked in the galley. I knew the captain and several of the crew. They saved my life!"

And Mr. Waldron, with a keen nose for news, was curious.

"I thought there was something very interesting about you; tell me how you came to know the crew of that ship and how they saved your life?"

"It's such a long story," said John, "it's such a long story."

"Don't worry about that; I have time if you have time to tell it."

While reading the article about the tragedy of the S.S. Bayano and its crew that he had come to know so well, the whole Cuban saga and his miraculous escape all came back to him, and he told the publisher his story. He left nothing out. He told him about his good fortune in getting the job in Cuba through Mr. Brewster, the UFC employment agent, and how he worked as a carpenter on the Banes plantation during the Zafra season in 1911-1912, of his visit with some Cuban co-workers in the town of La Maya when the race war against Afro Cubans broke out, how he and two other friends were trying to get back to Banes when they were ambushed on a train by blood-thirsty militiamen and soldiers and dragged off the train into the woods to be executed, how they attempted to escape, got separated, and one of his friends was killed while they were getting away in a boat, and how he was the only one who managed to escape in a small boat by sea and after a few days adrift alone on the Atlantic Ocean, how he was rescued by the crew of the S.S. Bayano and worked in the galley as an assistant chef for six months until they returned to Panama, and he was able to return to his Uncle who lived in Caledonia and who, along with his aunts in Jamaica, had feared that he might have died in Cuba, and how he got his present job as a super for Mr. Brewster taking care of his properties. It was an experience that he would never forget and that left a mark on his life. And now, the news of the S.S. Bayano being sunk…he could not express how sad it made him feel for the men to whom he owed his life.

While he was telling all this to him, Mr. Waldron, an experienced newspaperman, took it all down, for he was so moved he was determined to have the story published in the Workman. He got John's permission to publish the story and assured him that it would be of major human interest and people would want to read about it and would be moved, just as he was when they read it. He took his address down to contact him when the story was published to let him know and to send him a copy. After the details of the story were reviewed and written down, they continued a conversation about several local topics of interest.

"Stories like yours are interesting to my readers because it tells them how badly our people are treated and how they have to survive not only here in Panama but in places like Cuba."

"You mean everywhere we go, not just Cuba alone, for that matter," interjected John.

"Yes," said Mr. Waldron, "that's why I try to tell my people through my editorials how important it is for them to help each other right here in Panama, to unite as a people against injustices."

"Are you having any success in that effort?"

"I like to think that they realize what I am telling them is true; however, a lot of times they feel they can't do anything, that everybody and everything is against them."

"Who is to blame for that?" asked John.

"It's hard to blame them. First, the French and then the Americans made a lot of promises to them when they were recruiting and advertising to get workers to come to work on the canal, but they never told them the whole truth. They brought all these West Indians over here and treated them only slightly better than slaves, grossly underpaying them, with little or no benefits, no rights or voice, and now that the canal is finished, they have abandoned them and their 1st and 2nd generation descendants in the terminal cities of Colon and Panama, except for a few who were shipped back home, or who returned home on their own. Now, who do you think should be blamed? Tell me."

"I am no politician, sir, but it seems to me that when the French and the Americans were busy building this Eighth Wonder of the World, nobody was taking into account what they were going to do about all these West Indians and their descendants left here in this country afterward, especially the ones born here and in the Canal Zone."

"You are a genius, my son," said Mr. Waldron, "you hit the nail right on the head. The British abandoned us; the Panamanians don't want us, although they are glad for us to spend our hard-earned pay in their country; and the Americans oppress us with their racism and then discard us like worn-out shoes after exploiting our labor and loyalty, and they certainly don't want us. I tell you, it bleeds my heart to see what they do to our people."

"I don't envy your job as a newspaperman and as a crusader for justice; your paper can be an instrument for change if people want change and are willing to sacrifice to bring it about, but they are up against a three-headed monster here: The U.S. gov., the Panamanian gov., and the British gov. I wouldn't be in your shoes."

"Is that the best advice you can give to me? I thought you and I were on the same side?"

"Yes, we are. I was only pointing out what I am sure you already knew. There is one thing I am sure we are in total agreement on, and that is that we, as a people, must unite; it's the only way."

"Yes, and someday we will. Some day, we will. By the way, did I hear you say you were taking care of some buildings here in Colon, that you are a superintendent?"

"Yes, I am taking care of four buildings for the owner, 3 on 10th Street and 1 on 7th Street."

"In the history of Colon, there has been one major fire in 1885 when Panama was part of Columbia, and it almost burned down the whole city. There have been a few minor fires since, but what I am trying to say is that we haven't seen the last one yet, and there will continue to be more if something isn't done to prevent it."

"What do you mean there'll be more fires if something isn't done to prevent it?"

"Have you looked at the kind of housing structures we have in this city? Colon remains a fertile tinderbox, just waiting for a match to set it off. These wooden buildings have no serious protection against disaster by fire. And no City fire codes either. Tell me, what fire regulations do you have in your buildings? People go to sleep every night in these wooden structures and don't know what peril they are living in. Now, I don't want to alarm you, son, but that is something to think about, isn't it?"

He sure gave John Graham something to think about because he had to admit he was right: the city is not adequately protected against a possible conflagration, and he, John Graham, is working as a super for 4 firetraps.

"I think you are being a little pessimistic, Mr. Waldron. We'll be alright if we are very careful," he said dubiously.

"I hope you are right, son; in any case, it doesn't hurt to be aware of these things."

Before they parted company, Mr. Waldron thanked him for the article and told him it should be out in the next weekly issue of the Workman, and he wished him the best until the next time they see each other.

The article came out in the next Saturday issue as Mr. Waldron had promised, and John was proud to show it to his Marianne when he was with her that day in her apartment. She was obviously moved by it by her remarks.

"What a tragedy! I can't believe that you were there and were shot at! And you almost drowned in the ocean! O John, if you had died, we never would have met!" And she hugged him and kissed him.

"That's why I'm never going back to Cuba," said John, "I lost many good friends over there."

On Friday morning, April 30, 1915, Marianne was at work at the Cristobal commissary when she came down with a sudden illness. Her supervisor, seeing her distress and that she could not perform her duties, sent her home for the rest of the day. She went home, took a sedative, and went to lie down awhile. John was supposed to come by the apartment that night around 6 p.m., and she was hoping that she would feel better by then.

In the meantime, early that same morning, John had gone by Brewster's office to meet with him and to report on several things that needed to be done to the apartments in two of the buildings. Not to mention, he had also gone there to pick up his paycheck at the same time.

"Well, how are things coming along with those two apartments you were working on, John," said Mr. Brewster, "think they will be ready on time?"

"That's what I wanted to talk to you about, sir. The fixtures were supposed to have been delivered 2 days ago, and they still have not arrived. You might want to contact the supplier. Otherwise, they will not be ready on time for next week. In building 780 on 7th Street, the contractors have 1 day left to finish the ground floor space for the new offices scheduled to open next Wednesday, May 5th."

"Well, at least that's good news; I'll take care of the fixtures, and what about the tenant complaints? Are they keeping you busy? And your new assistant and the new help I gave you, how are they working out?"

"The tenants are alright, not too many complaints, and you know as well as I that there is enough to keep me busy all the time. It would be impossible to keep up with it without the new help. But there is something else I wanted to talk to you about."

"And what is that?" asked Mr. Brewster.

"Have you ever considered how vulnerable these buildings are without fire and safety building codes? And they are all made of wood, not just your buildings, I mean all of Colon with few exceptions."

"Are you getting squeamish about your job at this time?"

"No, sir, I like my job. I am thinking about my job, and I am looking out for your interest as well."

"I am following government building codes that exist, if any, just like all the other property owners; I am not looking to spend a lot of money to rebuild Colon on my own. The way I find it is fine if everybody else likes it that way, so long as there's a profit to be made. Besides, what suggestion did you have in mind anyway that's not going to cost me an arm and a leg?"

"I thought that we should post some fire and safety rules in the buildings for the tenants to follow and that maybe we could have a few fire extinguishers placed in the buildings as a safety measure, just in case. It doesn't hurt to safeguard your property in every way we can."

"The safety rules are fine, but if we purchase any fire extinguishers, that will mean I will have to increase the rent, you understand. Check out the cost and let me know so I can figure out how much to increase the rent. If there isn't anything else, I must be leaving in a minute to catch a train."

Their meeting came to an end, and John left the office to return to work. At about 3 p.m., Brewster was on the train bound for Panama City, and John was at 380 7th Street doing some last-minute repairs to get an apartment ready for a new tenant who was to move in the following Monday. Marianne, meanwhile, was at home in bed sleeping after taking a sedative and some cold medication to help her feel better.

At about 3:10 p.m., there was a big commotion in the street, and people were yelling, "FIRE! ...FIRE!" It caused John Graham to come outside to see what was going on. It was a big one, and there was no time to waste. He rushed back inside the building to get everyone out and to save what he could. Before anyone knew it, the fire was blazing across 1/3 of the city, and the hapless Colon fire brigade was unable to stop it. Of course, the Cristobal fire station had joined with the Colon firefighters to do what they could as it was threatening to burn down Cristobal as well. The fire started in Bottle Alley between 7th and 8th Streets and burned to 11th Street, destroying most of Front Street, damaging the PRR building, the commissary, the Masonic Temple building, and the Telephone Exchange Building. Then it passed 11th Street, burning southward between Bolivar and D Streets toward 14th Street before it was checked by explosives that were used to demolish some of the buildings to stop the spreading flames. In all, 22 blocks were burned to the ground, 10 people were killed, many injured, and tens of thousands were made homeless.

The next day, special editions were published in the Workman, the Colon Starlet, the Independence, and other local newspapers covering the fire. In one article, it was stated that this fire of April 30, 1915, was the second worst fire to date in Colon's history, and a theory was put forth as to how it started. It was believed by some that the fire was deliberately set by a person or persons who were determined to eradicate Colon's most shameful thoroughfare, its blatant red-light district, 'Bottle Alley,' where the most flourishing businesses were prostitution, gambling, and drinking; but the perpetrators' crazed disregard for public safety had taken down not only Bottle Alley but also more than 1/3 of the city, killing innocent people and making thousands homeless. In fact, the city now had to deal with a huge refugee crisis of tens of thousands of homeless and displaced people in need of immediate shelter, food, and other necessities.

Colon Fire 1915 (Google)

While the fire was raging, people were trying to save what personal belongings they could, if they could. John barely had time to rush back to 10th Street and salvage one small suitcase and a few personal items. In his mind, he believed that Marianne was safe in her job when the fire broke out. He did not know that she had returned home to her apartment on 9th street that morning, so he made his way to Cristobal's commissary to see if he could find her, only to be told, when he got there, that she had been sent home that morning due to illness; and that piece of news drove him into a panic. Did she get out in time? Was she safe? Was she rescued? He now rushed to every rescue station, to the hospital, to the police station, to find out if Marianne was accounted for.

Evaline, who worked in the hospital, went with him to the emergency ward to see if she was brought in, but her name was not on any list. They were told that there were only 10 fatalities in the fire, so of all the thousands of people who were saved, they had to believe that she was one of them and that they would find her somewhere alive. It was then that someone in the rescue squad heard Evaline and John inquiring about survivors from the building where her sister lived, and they told them the sad news about the body of a young woman that they had removed from that building just before it collapsed. Of all the worst possibilities, that body turned out to be Marianne's. She was one of the 10 unfortunate fatalities of the fire. The rescuers remembered when they arrived at her apartment, they had to break the door down, but it was too late; that in her sleep, the toxic smoke had overwhelmed her, probably as she tried to awaken, she was suffocated by the smoke. Sadly, her body was taken to the mortuary.

Over the next few weeks, Colon was still trying to grasp the nightmare; people were still looking for relatives and trying to find their way, businesses came to a standstill, bread lines were established, and a huge tent city to shelter the homeless was erected by the American military. The Panamanian government was trying to assess the causes and damages and debating how to prevent such a tragedy in the future. Consequently, President Belisario Porras later issued decree #23 on May 31, 1915, which provided in Article 1 that all buildings reconstructed and all new buildings in Colon should, from that date, be of masonry, brick, concrete, or other fireproof material.

In the meantime, the harshest reality John Graham came to realize was that the journalist W. N. Waldron was right in his prediction, and he realized, too, that it took such a tragedy to happen before the Panamanian government would attempt to do something about the fragile tinderbox called Colon City. Prophetic as it seemed, just that same morning, he had sat in his landlord boss Samuel Brewster's office complaining about the lack of adequate fire and safety codes and regulations throughout the city. But now, he didn't care anymore about that; he didn't care anything about anything now that they just started to address the problem because the personal cost to him was already far too great: it was too late to save the life of his beloved Marianne.

This tragedy was too much for him to take. He crucified himself for what happened. If only, he thought, if only he had known that she had returned to her apartment not feeling well that morning, if only they had not waited so long to get married.

If only he had gone to her place first when the fire broke out instead of to her job. But who could have known what was on the cards that day? Hindsight is a brute and an awfully cruel teacher. Now, all his hopes and plans of ever marrying and settling down with Marianne were dashed forever.

He helped Evaline with the arrangements, and the church, which fortunately was still standing after the fire, had a service for her followed by an interment. Evaline found a place to stay with a co-worker, and John returned to Caledonia, where a friend of his uncle's offered him a temporary place to stay until he got back on his feet. He had notified Mr. Brewster, whose houses had all burned down and who seemed to take the losses in stride.

"I will rise again," he said to John, "when Colon is built back up. If you want to hang around, in about six months or so, I will rebuild from the ashes and have a job waiting for you."

"I don't think so," said John, "I've lost all interest in Panama now; I'm going back home to Jamaica."

He had lived through too many tragedies and near tragedies, enough to sour the once bright outlook of a happy Trench Town boy in search of adventure. The sudden death of his father; the dynamite explosion in Culebra that killed a worker he just shared lunch with; the race war in Cuba that cost thousands of lives, including his Cuban friends; his close call with death by the militia; his near perishing while adrift on the Atlantic Ocean; the death of the entire crew of the steamship Bayano who had saved his life, all bore heavily on him, and, finally, the dreadful fire in Colon that took the life of his beloved Marianne was the last straw that he could bear. He wrote aunts Sarah and Beulah and Uncle Cyrus and told them he was through with adventures; he was through with Panama, and he was coming home. He booked passage on a UFC ship, and on June 17, 1915, he sailed back home to Jamaica.

When he arrived, Aunts Sarah and Beulah and Uncle Cyrus were waiting to meet him at the pier in Kingston, and Aunts Sarah and Beulah were astonished when they saw him. Not only had he grown a few inches taller, but his whole demeanor had changed. He looked gaunt, so much older, sadder, and frail for a twenty-two-year-old young man. Even his hair had greyed a little. He left Jamaica only five years ago, but he had aged so much in that short time. The joy and exuberance of youth were gone forever; there was now a marked seriousness in his face and sadness that only comes from experiencing life's harshest realities that leave their silent wounds and inner scars. He left home a happy, innocent boy, and he returned a broken, saddened, hardened, scarred, and prematurely aged man who had lost the joy of life.

www.ingramcontent.com/pod-product-compliance
Lightning Source LLC
Chambersburg PA
CBHW040910010826
48978CB00013BB/1229